SIERRA JENS

Take My Hand

ROBIN JONES GUNN

BETHANY HOUSE PUBLISHERS
MINNEAPOLIS, MINNESOTA 55438

Take My Hand
Copyright © 1999
Robin Jones Gunn

Edited by Janet Kobobel Grant
Cover design by Praco, Ltd. Cover illustration by Angelo Tillary

A Focus on the Family book published by
Bethany House Publishers
A Ministry of Bethany Fellowship International
11400 Hampshire Avenue South
Minneapolis, Minnesota 55438
www.bethanyhouse.com

Printed in the United States of America by
Bethany Press International, Minneapolis, Minnesota 55438

Library of Congress Cataloging-in-Publication Data

Gunn, Robin Jones, 1955–
    Take my hand / Robin Jones Gunn.
      p.   cm. — (The Sierra Jensen series; 12)
    Summary: On a trip to Southern California, Sierra has a rocky reunion with her love interest, Paul, whom she has not seen in more than a year, and feels confusion yet again about their future.
    ISBN 1–56179–736–7
    [1. Interpersonal relations—Fiction. 2. Christian life—Fiction.
3. California, Southern—Fiction.] I. Title. II. Series: Gunn, Robin Jones, 1955–   Sierra Jensen series; 12.
PZ7.G972Tak   1999
[Fic]—dc21   98–55512
                                            CIP
                                            AC

99 00 01 02 03 04 05 / 15 14 13 12 11 10 9 8 7 6 5 4 3 2 1

To Tiffany, Michele, and Nicole,
three precious, peculiar treasures.
Don't ever lose the love
you feel for Him now.

chapter one

SIERRA JENSEN BENT DOWN AND LIFTED THE DUST ruffle, taking one last look under her bed. Not even a dust bunny greeted her. The space was clean and cleared out, just like the rest of her bedroom.

Sierra sat up and for a brief moment admired the rare view. The warm breezes of the late August afternoon pushed their way past the sheer curtains, compelling them to hop out of the way. Then racing around the room, past the antique dresser with the oval mirror, the overstuffed chair, and the two twin beds made up with ivory chenille bedspreads, the breezes found nothing out of place to disrupt and flew out the door and down the hallway of the old Victorian house.

Sierra's bedroom had never been so orderly—except maybe when her family moved to Portland the middle of her junior year of high school. She had been in England the week they moved, and when she first had stepped into this room, it looked this tidy. But that tidiness was due to her older sister, Tawni, who had been the one to put everything in its place.

Now Sierra was all packed and leaving for college. Tawni had moved out a year ago and last week had announced her engagement to Jeremy. It seemed only a blink of time since their family had moved here, and a sudden sadness swept over Sierra as another rush of late summer breezes muscled their way through the screen on the second-story window and rushed around her room.

"Is that everything?" Sierra's mom asked, stepping in from the hallway. She must have read the wistful look on Sierra's face because, with a knowing smile, Mrs. Jensen came over and sat down next to her daughter on the edge of the bed.

"Where did it go?" Sierra asked quietly.

"Did you lose something?" her mom asked.

Sierra sighed. "My childhood. It was here a minute ago."

Mrs. Jensen laughed softly and slipped her arm around Sierra's shoulders. "I know, honey. Believe me, I know."

"What if I want it back?"

"Sorry. It's on to the next step."

"But what if I really mess up?" Sierra said. "What if I turn out to be really bad at being responsible?"

Mrs. Jensen laughed again.

"What if I'm not cut out for college life?"

"What would you rather do?"

"I don't know. Travel, maybe. Go live in Europe for a while. Sail the seven seas. Hike Mount Fuji."

"You can do all those things as long as . . ." Mrs. Jensen paused.

"As long as I go to college first, right?"

"No, I was going to say, as long as you ask your Father."

"Ask Dad?" Sierra said, giving her mother a questioning look.

Mrs. Jensen pointed upward. "No, your heavenly

Father. You have no idea yet what amazing adventures lie ahead of you in adulthood. God, on the other hand, has your future all planned out. So get used to asking Him. Always. About everything. He'll lead you, Sierra."

Quietly, Sierra added, "He'll lead me like the Good Shepherd that He is." She felt a warmth come over her at the memory of Paul's words from a letter he had written to her months ago. It was the last letter he had written before he left Scotland, and he had talked about God being the Good Shepherd who cares for and protects His sheep. Thinking about that made the future seem less terrifying. How could it be frightening when God had already been there?

Sierra jumped up from the bed as her startled mother looked at her.

"Oh no! What time is it? I'm supposed to meet Amy and Vicki at Mama Bear's. I almost forgot, and I'm probably already late," Sierra said.

"Oh." Mrs. Jensen rose and glanced around the room. "You have everything ready, I see. Did Wes pack those last two boxes into the trailer?"

"He took them down. I don't know if they fit." Sierra felt a little funny about the melancholy moment she had just had with her mom. After all, Sierra's older brother Wes was going to the same university she was attending in Southern California: Rancho Corona. Wes had graduated from Oregon State University. Now he was going on for his master's at Rancho Corona. And Tawni lived less than an hour's drive from the college. Sierra wasn't sure why she had suddenly felt so sad about leaving. It wasn't as if she were leaving all her family and friends.

Actually, she was going to be with most of her closest

friends when she went to college. Vicki and Randy were flying to Southern California the next weekend and had brought over a lot of their belongings the night before so Sierra's dad and Wes could pack them in the rented trailer that was hooked up to the Jensen family van.

Tomorrow, Friday, in the morning, Sierra, Mr. Jensen, Wes, and Sierra's two youngest brothers, Gavin and Dillon, would leave for the two-day road trip. Mrs. Jensen would fly down on Saturday with Granna Mae, with whom the family lived. They would all gather in San Diego for Tawni's big engagement party.

"I have to run," Sierra told her mom, dashing down the stairs. "I'll be back soon. If Paul phones, tell him to call back after 8:00. Is it okay if I take your car?"

Mrs. Jensen stood at the top of the stairs. When Sierra turned to look to her for an answer, she thought her mom was the one who looked wistful now. Their mother-daughter moment had been cut short.

"Sure. Have a good time. The keys are on the hook in the kitchen."

At moments like this Sierra most admired her mom. Sometimes Sierra wondered if her mom had been blessed with an extra-sensitive memory so that she remembered what it was like to be 17 and to have friends who were almost more important than family, and feelings that were almost overwhelming. Certainly she knew what Sierra was feeling now because she let Sierra go rather than try to extend their time together.

The screen door slammed behind Sierra as she went out the back door. Her dad and Wes were still reconfiguring the jigsaw puzzle of boxes that needed to be loaded into the trailer.

"Lots of junk, huh?" Sierra said.

"It's not junk," Wesley corrected her. "You'll find these few worldly possessions are your favorite treasures once you get to school."

Mr. Jensen took a swig from the soft drink can he held. The late afternoon sun hit the top of his head just right, highlighting the perspiration beaded up where his hairline was receding. "It's all this band equipment that Randy wants to send with us that's not exactly fitting into the trailer."

"He said it was okay if you couldn't fit it in, didn't he?" Sierra said. Randy and some of his friends had started a band that had pretty much fallen apart by midsummer. Sierra knew that Randy was bringing along all the band equipment only because he owned it, not because he necessarily needed it. "I mean, if you can't fit it in, you can't." Sierra rolled up the sleeves of her long, white cotton shirt. It was actually one of her dad's old shirts, which she had put on over her shorts and tank top when she was packing stuff that morning. All the windows had been open, and the air had been cool then. Somehow, having her dad's shirtsleeves around her as she packed and cleaned had been comforting, and so Sierra had left it on.

"Oh, we'll get it in somehow," Mr. Jensen said. "You might be sitting on a few duffel bags in the van for the next two days, but we'll get it all in."

"I'm going to Mama Bear's," Sierra said, pulling her long, curly, blonde hair up in a clip she had just discovered in her shirt's pocket. She had stuck it there a few hours ago and then, forgetting where she had put it, had wasted 20 minutes going through her packed luggage trying to find it when her room started to heat up.

"Hey, buy some cinnamon rolls for tomorrow's breakfast," Mr. Jensen said. He reached into his pocket to pull out a money clip.

"I've got it," Sierra said, patting the small wallet pouch she had tucked in her back pocket. "My treat."

Mr. Jensen smiled one of his crinkles-around-the-corners-of-the-eyes smiles. He didn't have to say any words. That look told Sierra he was proud of her and he loved her.

She turned away quickly before the sensation of her father's loving glance could work its way to the center of her tender heart. She opened the door of her mom's new white sedan and slid across the seat. It was actually a used car but new to Mrs. Jensen. Just three days ago they had traded in the old Volkswagen Rabbit that Sierra had shared with her mom for the past year. Several months ago, her parents had given the car to Sierra, but that meant she was responsible for her own insurance payments and for all the gas she used.

It wasn't hard for her to decide not to take the car with her to college. She had worked out a good deal with her parents when they said they would buy it back from her. Sierra now had enough spending money to make it through at least the first semester, so she wouldn't have to find a job right away.

Wesley had done the same thing, selling his finicky sports car and pocketing the profit. Several friends who were going to Rancho had assured Sierra and Wes that those with cars would help those without get around. Their friends also told them that the public transportation in that area was much more convenient than in most parts of Southern California.

As Sierra drove the short city blocks to the bakery where she had worked the past year and a half, she felt another wave of memories. This older part of town had become so familiar. She remembered so many amazing and frustrating things that had happened here, such as the time they thought Granna Mae had wandered away from home in one of her forgetful states and they had combed the area looking for her. Or the time Sierra had marched down the street to the mailbox, where she mailed her first brazen letter to Paul, telling him exactly what she thought of him.

That memory brought an irrepressible smile. She and Paul had come so far in their relationship since that first communication, when he had teasingly called her the "Daffodil Queen." Then the term had insulted her. Now it warmed her. Daffodil Queen was Paul's nickname for her, and when he called her that over the phone during one of their conversations, she always melted inside.

Still smiling, Sierra cautiously parallel-parked her mom's car along the busy street in the Hawthorne District, a few blocks from Mama Bear's. This was about the same spot where Paul had driven by her as she walked one rainy day, carrying an armful of daffodils home to Granna Mae, who was recovering from surgery. Now, as Sierra stepped from the car and made sure she had locked all the doors, she thought of how right here, on this sidewalk, the Daffodil Queen legend had begun.

She stood still for a moment, feeling the intense summer sun beat down on her shoulders. Cars roared past, shoppers bobbed in and out of the unique shops, a guy wearing dark blue knee pads jogged by with a very young golden retriever on a short leash. But Sierra stood still, eager to remember every sight and sound. Tomorrow she would leave all this and start the next chapter in her life.

Reaching instinctively, as she had countless times, for the long silver chain around her neck, Sierra felt the shape of the silver daffodil that hung at the end of the necklace. It had been Paul's graduation present to her in June and her only link to him all summer. The sporadic phone calls and few letters didn't carry the same meaning as this necklace did. This was a gift from his heart, a daffodil he had had made for her by a jeweler in Scotland. Whenever Sierra held it like this, it was as if she were holding Paul's hand. In two short days, she would exchange the cool silver touch of the daffodil for the warm grasp of Paul's hand, because in two days she would see him face-to-face for the first time in more than a year.

chapter two

*S*IERRA BIT HER LOWER LIP AND FORCED HERSELF TO move toward the bakery, where her friends were certainly waiting for her by now. Vicki, Amy, and she had met there once a week for months. They would bend their heads close, open their hearts wide, and lower their voices to levels at which only true friends dare listen in. This last meeting was going to be awful.

The bell above the door of Mama Bear's Bakery chimed merrily, as if today were any other day. Sierra had heard that bell at least a million times, she estimated. Today was the first time the sound brought tears to her eyes.

Blinking quickly and forcing herself to look at the familiar table by the window, Sierra saw Amy and Vicki in the thick of conversation and unaware that Sierra had entered. She took advantage of the moment and went to the counter, where her dear-hearted boss, Mrs. Kraus, was ringing up an order.

Sierra stood in line behind a dark-haired woman with a toddler balanced on her hip. Bending her first two fingers in a friendly wave at the boy, Sierra smiled at him. He turned away, burying his face in his mommy's shoulder, but only for a minute before shyly emerging and examining

Sierra with serious gray eyes. The toddler then turned his head to the side and gave Sierra an adorable smile that she couldn't help but return.

What a little doll! Sierra thought. *If I were responsible for raising him and if he ever gave me one of those grins when I was about to say no, I'm afraid I couldn't deny him anything.*

She waved again and offered her most engaging smile. The boy kept smiling at her.

Just then the woman carrying him turned to see what had captured the child's attention, and when she turned, Sierra recognized her immediately.

"Jalene," she said without thinking.

Jalene looked closely at Sierra, raising one thin, dark eyebrow in an obvious sign of nonrecognition.

"Jalene," Sierra said again, having a hard time formulating her thoughts. "Hi."

"I'm sorry," Jalene said coolly. "Have we met before?" She had fine, dark facial features, and her hair wasn't as short and jet black as it used to be. Sierra remembered the catlike smile that had curved up Jalene's lips when Sierra first had seen her almost two years ago. But Jalene's lips weren't smiling now.

"No, we haven't met. I'm Sierra. Sierra Jensen."

Jalene still looked confused. The toddler on her hip had lost his smile now, too.

Sierra let out a nervous laugh and wished she had kept her mouth shut for once. Now she needed to explain. "I'm Paul's . . . I mean, I know Paul. Paul MacKenzie."

Jalene's eyes widened, but her smile still didn't come.

"He, um, I mean I . . . well, we met in England, and actually we were on the same plane when he was coming back from his grandfather's funeral. I saw you at the airport when you picked him up. That's how I know who you are. Paul told me. Your name, I mean. Paul told me you were picking him up."

A faint recognition came across Jalene's face.

Sierra laughed again nervously. "As a matter of fact, I loaned Paul the money to call you from London. He didn't have enough change, and I was waiting to use the phone, and . . . well, that's kind of how we met."

Jalene shifted the toddler to her other hip. "And Paul and you are together now?"

Sierra had no idea how to answer that. She and Paul hadn't defined their relationship. How could she summarize it for Jalene? Her pause and probably her involuntary facial expression must have told Jalene more than her careful explanation. "Well, my sister is engaged to Paul's brother, and so that's kind of the connection."

"Oh."

Panic washed over Sierra faster than she could compose herself. She wanted to run into the bathroom and hide her face from this scrutinizing former girlfriend of Paul's. She didn't trust her tongue not to slip and say something ridiculous, like how she had ended up at Paul's old college accidentally one day and how she had seen Jalene at the gas station and then again in the parking lot and had watched her secretly and that's really why Sierra recognized her.

It felt bizarre to be face-to-face with this woman. This was the girlfriend Sierra had prayed Paul would break up with. And when they did break up, Paul had told Sierra his mother thought Sierra was an angel for praying so diligently. Sierra literally bit her tongue so she wouldn't slip up and blurt out to Jalene that Sierra's earnest prayers had quite possibly contributed to Paul and Jalene's breakup.

"Well," Jalene said after an awkward pause had paralyzed both of them long enough. "Nice meeting you. Tell Paul I said hello when you see him."

Sierra nodded and tried to smile naturally. "Okay" was the only word she let slip out of her mouth.

Jalene adjusted the little boy on her hip and lifted the white bag of warm cinnamon rolls from where Mrs. Kraus had placed them on the counter before going into the back. Two more customers had entered the shop, and now Sierra was at the front of the line. Sierra started to turn away from Jalene but felt the woman's dark eyes holding her longer than necessary in their examination.

The cat smile never came to Jalene's lips. But the little boy in her arms made up for her coolness by granting Sierra one more heart-melting grin from his tilted head. Sierra waved good-bye to him, and Jalene turned and walked out of the bakery without looking back.

"Ready for some tea, dear?" Mrs. Kraus asked when Sierra finally turned to greet her. "The girls have already picked up their tea and roll."

"Yes. I'd like to have some peppermint tea, if you have any more. I know we were out last Monday."

"I just received my tea shipments yesterday," Mrs. Kraus said. "And this is my treat. Vicki told me it was the last time for you three. I'd like to treat all of you."

"That's so sweet of you. Thanks. I also want a dozen cinnamon rolls before I go home, and those I want to pay for. It's for breakfast tomorrow before we hit the road."

"You let me know when you're ready to leave, and I'll

have them packed up for you." Mrs. Kraus stepped away from the register to fill a little ceramic teapot with boiling water. Sierra looked down at the familiar counter with the tip jar next to the register. The jar had sat on the counter ever since Sierra had worked at Mama Bear's and had a handwritten sign taped to it. The sign read, "If you fear change, leave it here." And the jar was always filled with change.

Sierra pulled a five-dollar bill from her pouch and tucked it into the change jar. Yes, it was symbolic of how she feared this change in her life, but it was also the least she could do for dear Mrs. Kraus, who had done so much for her. The world had never seen a more kind-hearted boss, and Sierra knew she would probably never again have such an enjoyable job with such a flexible schedule.

Smiling her thanks when Mrs. Kraus handed her the teapot and cup with the peppermint tea bag, Sierra realized her tongue was sore. Probably from biting it too long while she was trying not to slip up around Jalene. Sierra walked over to the window table, swishing her tongue from side to side and then sticking it out to make sure it wasn't swollen.

"Oh, well, that's real attractive," Vicki said, watching Sierra approach them.

Sierra made a goofy face, and Vicki and Amy both smiled.

Smiling is a good way to start this time together, Sierra thought. *I don't know if I'm up for how things will most likely end.*

"Who were you talking to at the counter?" Amy asked. She was the analytical one of the trio, and Sierra wondered for a moment how much she wanted to say. Amy's steady, dark eyes locked in on Sierra's blue-gray ones and seemed to pull Sierra's free spirit down to the table, where all secrets were shared openly.

Sierra took her time, sitting down and dunking her tea bag in the pot. She could feel Vicki staring at her, too, waiting for an explanation. Whereas Amy attracted attention because of her short, wavy, dark hair and dramatic Italian looks, Vicki was even more attractive. She was, in fact, stunning. Her long, straight, brown hair hung like silk from a center part, and her light green eyes were set like precious stones in her perfectly balanced face. Both of these friends had intimidated Sierra more than once with their piercing looks, and she knew if she glanced up from her teapot, they would both do it to her again.

So she didn't look up. She poured the tea into her cup and answered while gazing at her reflection in the steaming tea. "That was Jalene, Paul's old girlfriend."

"Really?" Vicki said.

"Why does stuff like that always happen to you?" Amy said. "I mean, what are the chances of your seeing her today, of all days, when you're about to see Paul?"

"I don't know," Sierra said, looking up. Her dad had often teased her when crazy things happened by muttering, "Only you, Sierra. Only you." It seemed now that Amy was about to join him in his muttering.

"Nothing ever happens just because it happens," Vicki philosophized. "We've said that before, here at this very table. God-things are all around us. Every day. We just don't always know at the time why they're happening."

"Do you suppose," Amy said quietly, leaning forward, "that God wanted you to see her and know that she was married and had a baby and everything so that you could tell Paul, and he would definitely be over her?"

"I think he is over her. Long over. He's never said anything about her," Sierra said.

"Why would he?" Vicki asked.

"Did she ask about him?" Amy probed.

"No, not really. She just told me to say hi to him when I saw him."

"So she knows you and Paul are together," Amy said.

"No, not really. I mean, I didn't say we were."

"Why not?" Amy asked.

Sierra looked at Amy and then at Vicki. All she could do was shrug. "Because I don't know if we are together. Not really. I mean, nothing has been defined."

"Well, it'll sure be defined by Saturday when you see him," Amy said. "And I hope you know it's killing me that I'm not going to be there to hear all about it."

The same sadness that had been blowing over Sierra all afternoon rushed over her once more. Sierra and Vicki were going to be roommates at Rancho Corona University, but Amy wasn't going to college with them. She had applied at the beginning of the summer but couldn't attend because of finances. Her parents were recently divorced, and she hadn't applied for financial aid soon enough. The three friends had been excited when Amy had decided to apply to Rancho, so when she was turned down, they were devastated. They had formulated a plan for Amy to take classes at the community college and work as many hours as she could at her uncle's restaurant. By next semester they figured she would be able to attend Rancho.

"Just promise you'll call me or E-mail as soon as you can and tell me all about it," Amy said. Sierra could tell Amy was trying to be brave about everything.

"I'll still be here next week," Vicki said. "At least the first part of the week. So when Sierra calls you, then you call me and tell me everything. Okay?"

Amy nodded courageously. Vicki shot a glance at Sierra. Sierra couldn't help it; tears were pooling at the corners of her eyes. All it took was the infallible law of gravity to pull them down her cheeks. For the next 15 minutes, the three friends cried together.

chapter three

SIERRA DECIDED IT ACTUALLY FELT GOOD TO BE ON the road the next day. The steady bump-bumping of the tires as the van and trailer sped down the freeway meant she was done saying good-bye for a while. She was on her way to see Paul. The sadness could leave her now. She could concentrate on all the wonderful things ahead of her.

But instead of concentrating on anything, all she wanted to do was sleep. She had been up nearly all night, even though she hadn't planned on it. After the meeting time at Mama Bear's, Amy, Vicki, and Sierra had decided to go to Randy's house. Some other guys were over there when the girls arrived, and they all sat around looking at Randy's yearbook, reminiscing about the good times they had had together at Royal Academy and complaining about how all they had done that summer was work. Sierra agreed that if she had it to do over again, she would have taken a little more time off from work instead of volunteering for everyone else's vacation hours. She would have done something fun, like backpacking with the youth group the way she had the summer before.

The unofficial end-of-the-summer party stretched into

the night, and Sierra had called her parents to get permission to stay later than her curfew. Her mom had said that Paul hadn't called, so Sierra felt no need to rush home. Once again, Mrs. Jensen seemed to understand how important this last good-bye was for Sierra.

By the time she left Randy's house, Sierra had hugged and cried and said good-bye one too many times. All she wanted to do was go home and crash. But when she got home, she found a note on her pillow from her dad saying they would be leaving early. They pulled out of the driveway at 4:00 in the morning, which meant Sierra had managed to squeeze in only a few hours of sleep.

Now that they were well on their way, she tried to catch up on those missing hours of rest. The van's motion cooperated with her goal, but her two little brothers didn't. Gavin and Dillon slept only the first hour or so, waking up when Mr. Jensen stopped for a rest-room break in Eugene. Now the seven- and nine-year-old boys were wide awake and making sure everyone else was, too.

Sierra had made a little nest for herself on the backseat of the van with the extra duffel bags. What she wished she had were tiny duffel bags to stuff in her ears to block out her brothers' noise. She and Wesley had made this same trek earlier that spring, when they drove down with Amy, Randy, and Vicki to check out Rancho Corona. What a different experience that had been!

More than ever, Sierra was looking forward to being on her own, away from her siblings and in the company of her friends. She didn't know if she should feel guilty for such thoughts or if it was a natural part of growing up and leaving home.

Drifting into a restless sleep, Sierra tried to refresh her

thrashed emotions. She knew for certain she needed them to be intact when she arrived in San Diego the next day.

For a good part of the trip, Sierra did rest. Not deeply or comfortably, but she kept to herself and pretended to be asleep a lot more than she really was. Many times she turned down pleas from Gavin and Dillon to play a game with them. When Wes tried to convince her to trade places with him when he wasn't driving, she reluctantly gave in. Instead of providing interesting conversation for her dad, she simply stuffed her pillow between herself and the door and tried to get comfortable enough around the shoulder-strap seat belt so she could sleep.

What Sierra was really doing, while appearing to be sleeping, was daydreaming about seeing Paul. By the second afternoon of the trip, she had pretty much decided to run into Paul's arms and hug him, regardless of who was around. That was, she decided, the true expression of her feelings for him, and she shouldn't hold back. She played the possible angles over and over in her mind. What would she wear? What would Paul be doing when she saw him? Who would be watching them?

Only a few times did the caution alarms go off in Sierra's psyche. She had gotten carried away with emotional daydreams almost a year ago when she had read more into Paul's letters than was actually there. But this was different. He had given her a necklace. He had a nickname for her. He said he was looking forward to seeing her. Surely she hadn't exaggerated any of the feelings between them this time. She felt certain running into his arms and hugging him wouldn't be an overdone response.

Then, while they were stuck in traffic somewhere south of Los Angeles, the van's air conditioner quit. The thick, smoggy, late-summer heat bulldozed into the van as soon as they rolled down the windows. Within three minutes in the sluggish traffic, they were all hot and grouchy.

Mr. Jensen pulled off the freeway and drove into a gas station. They spent a miserable 40 minutes there only to find out the problem couldn't be fixed. At least not there and not then.

"We have to get on our way," Mr. Jensen said. "We'll just have to endure life without air conditioning and pretend we're pioneers."

"Pioneers?" Sierra questioned. She knew she wasn't trying very hard to be cooperative or cheerful in the midst of this annoyance. If she had been with her friends, she would have been Little Miss Mary Sunshine telling everyone else to cheer up. The truth about herself bothered her—and made her even grumpier.

Crawling into the extreme heat of her backseat nest, Sierra insisted they keep the side vented windows open even though the left one rattled terribly. "It's just too hot to close it," she said. "You guys have to leave it open, or I'll suffocate back here."

She tried to sleep. It was impossible. She sat up and tried to position herself so the most breeze came her way. That proved futile. So much traffic was on the freeway that the van wasn't going much faster than 25 miles per hour, which was hardly enough to whip up a respectable breeze.

All Sierra wanted to do was reach their destination. She drank the last bottle of water from their ice chest and half an hour later begged Gavin to give her some ice.

Sierra leaned over the seat, waiting for her brother to pull a handful of ice from the chest and give it to her so she could rub it over her neck and cool herself down. Gavin scrounged in the small ice chest between the front two seats and said, "Hey, you can have this!" In a jerking motion, Gavin shot up, snapped his arm around, and attempted to offer Sierra the last can of root beer he had found at the bottom of the ice chest. But Sierra had moved forward while Gavin scrounged in the ice, and her face was in his line of fire. Before she could see it coming, Gavin's fist and the cold can of root beer crashed into her face, hitting her under her left eye, right on the cheekbone.

Sierra let out such a shriek Mr. Jensen slammed on the brakes. Wes quickly assessed the situation and began to give direction, telling his dad to keep driving, telling Sierra to stop screaming, and telling Gavin to put his seat belt back on.

"I didn't mean it! I didn't mean it!" Gavin kept shouting.

"I know," Sierra shouted back. She didn't mean to shout, but in the midst of a painful black eye in the making, she found it nearly impossible to respond with anything lower than a yell.

"She knows it was an accident, Gavin," Wesley said calmly. "Don't worry. You didn't do anything wrong. You were trying to be nice and give her the last soda. It's okay."

Despite Wesley's calming words, Gavin was crying as if he were the one who had just gotten clobbered. Sierra was crying, too, more from frustration than pain. She knew by the way her face was throbbing that she was going to have a doozy of a black eye.

Wonderful. Just wonderful, she thought as her eyes smarted with tears. *The perfect way to show up on Paul's doorstep. I can't believe this happened to me! Go ahead, Dad,*

*say it. "Only you, Sierra. Something like this would only
happen to you."*

Her dad wasn't saying anything. He was trying to
change lanes without much success, and Sierra could see
his aggravated expression in the rearview mirror. Wesley
was directing him from instructions he had on a piece of
paper. She knew the best thing to do was to sit back and
not create any more trauma for the group.

Taking a deep breath, Sierra picked up the cold can of
root beer that had fallen onto the seat. She pressed it to
her cheek, hoping the cold would at least keep the swelling
down. A minute later she realized with irony that she was
cooling off. The can was extremely cold, almost too cold
to hold directly against her skin. That, plus the receding
burst of adrenaline, cooled her off.

"Gavin," Sierra said calmly.

He turned around and cautiously looked at her with
moist eyes. For a moment he reminded her of the charming
little boy Jalene had been holding at the bakery. All Sierra's
frustration dissolved.

"Gavin, please don't feel bad. I know you didn't mean
to do it. Wesley was right. You were being nice to me. It
was an accident. So don't feel bad about it anymore, okay?"

Gavin nodded and said, "Okay."

Dillon, who had been watching the fiasco with the
fascination of an onlooker at an accident, said, "Can we
see it?"

Sierra pulled away the can. She could feel her eye's
lower lid swelling despite the cold compress. Several years
ago, Sierra had accidentaly knocked out a janitor at an
airport with only a can of orange juice in her hand. She
now knew how the stunned janitor felt when she had

moved closer to him for an examination of his bruise.

Dillon made a gruesome face. "There's blood," he announced.

Sierra touched the thin portion of skin at the corner of her eye, and indeed there was blood. Only a drop, and it felt as if the tiny tear had already closed up. Definitely not a cause for panic or for stitches. "It's okay," Sierra said, returning the cold can to her throbbing eye.

"It's on your shirt, too," Dillon announced.

Sierra looked down, and sure enough, the white T-shirt she had saved for today so she would look fresh when she saw Paul and hugged him had a splattering of red drips down the left side. It looked as if a dizzy bird had dipped its feet in red paint and tried to walk down her shirt.

Sierra calmly assessed the situation. Or at least she *tried* to calmly assess the situation. They were a couple of hours away from San Diego by her calculations. That would give the swelling around her eye time to go down. Certainly they would need gas or someone would need to go to the bathroom before they arrived in San Diego. Then she could persuade her dad to open the back of the trailer, and somehow she would find her bag and a clean shirt. The duffel bag under her feet held only dirty clothes from the last two days.

With another rush of sadness, Sierra realized she couldn't simply take her bloody shirt home and ask her mother to remove the stain. From now on, Sierra was responsible for all her laundry. The realization sobered her and for some reason made her eye hurt more.

Then, to her surprise, her dad pulled off the freeway. She hoped it would be the gas stop she was counting on, but she didn't want to bug him about opening the jam-packed trailer until they actually stopped. The problem was he didn't stop. He followed Wesley's directions, weaving through a residential area until they came to a large house with a blue tile roof and a long driveway. That's when Mr. Jensen stopped the car.

"We're here!" he announced, smiling at Sierra in the rearview mirror.

chapter four

"HOW CAN WE BE HERE?" SIERRA SQUAWKED, removing the can from her eye and staring at her father. "This isn't San Diego. Paul's family doesn't live in a big, fancy house overlooking the beach."

Mr. Jensen turned around to view Sierra's eye. He winced slightly, and she began to wonder just how bad her injury was. "This is Lindy's parents' home," he explained.

All three of Sierra's brothers were already out of the car and headed for the front door.

"Lindy?" Sierra echoed, placing the can back on her eye.

"Lindy MacKenzie. Paul and Jeremy's mom. Didn't you hear the plans for this weekend?"

Sierra shook her head.

"Lindy's parents offered to have the engagement party here and let all of us stay with them because they have more room than the MacKenzies do. That way we don't have to rent a hotel room."

"How long will we be here?" Sierra asked, feeling lost and out of the loop for all the weekend plans.

"Tawni and Jeremy are at the airport right about now

picking up Mom and Granna Mae. We'll stay here tonight and tomorrow night. Tonight is dinner with the two families, and tomorrow is a reception at the MacKenzies' church in San Diego. On Monday I'll take you and Wes to Rancho and get you all set up. Don't you remember our discussing any of this?"

Sierra shook her head again.

"Let me see your eye." Mr. Jensen leaned closer and made a sympathetic sound with his tongue behind his teeth. "Let's get you in the house and see if we can find a better compress. You're going to have a nasty shiner."

"Great," Sierra muttered. She peeled her sweaty legs off the seat and the mound of duffel bags and crawled out of the van. At least it was cooler outside, with a nice ocean breeze blowing. And it felt good to stretch. But she felt fear, embarrassment, and excitement over seeing Paul. She glanced at the house's front door, which was now shut. Her brothers apparently had disappeared inside. Did that mean Paul knew she was here and was waiting for her to go all the way to the front door before he greeted her? What would be so hard about his coming halfway or even all the way out to the car? How could she run into his arms and hug him if he wouldn't even come out of the house? But then again, how graceful would it be to run into his arms with a can of root beer held fast to her face, hiding her hideous eye? Maybe it was better that he hadn't come out to the car. Maybe it would be darker inside. The bloodstains might not look so bad inside the house.

Sierra and her father walked up to the front door and rang the doorbell. Sierra kept her head down. She noticed the large clay pot by the front door full of bright yellow flowers with little blue flowers brimming over the edges and trickling down the sides.

The door opened, and a large woman with short, stylish white hair and large, light-blue-rimmed glasses welcomed them in. She was older than Sierra's mom and younger than Granna Mae, based on Sierra's one-second evaluation. The woman wore a gold charm bracelet that clinked pleasantly as she waved Sierra and her dad into the narrow entryway.

"Please, please, come on in. The boys wanted to go right out to the back to see the view. I haven't met you yet, Sierra. I'm Jeremy's grandmother. Please call me Catherine." The gracious woman smiled, revealing unusually white teeth. They weren't perfectly straight, but they were so white they were pretty when she smiled. She was young for a grandmother. Sierra could never imagine her grandmother inviting anyone to call her "Mae."

"How was the trip, Howard?" Catherine asked, motioning with her charm-braceleted hand for them to come into the sunken living room, which was two steps down from the entryway.

Sierra followed her dad. Two things bothered her. First, she was walking around with a can of root beer pressed against her face and Catherine hadn't even blinked. And second, where was Paul?

"Please sit down. May I bring you something to drink, or . . ." For the first time Catherine seemed to notice Sierra wasn't sipping from the can of soda in her hand.

Sierra slowly pulled down her hand to reveal her wound.

"Oh, gracious!" Catherine said. "You come into the kitchen with me, and we'll get a proper bag of ice on that. Goodness gracious! What happened?"

Fortunately, Mr. Jensen followed Sierra into the kitchen and explained the situation. He also took over the preparation of the compress by suggesting they use a small bag of frozen peas wrapped in a dish towel. It felt much better than the can of root beer.

"So, where's everyone else?" Sierra asked, trying to sound casual and trying to look natural with a bag of frozen peas covering the left side of her face.

"My husband is out back with the boys. Tawni and Jeremy went to the airport to pick up your mom and grandmother, and I expect Paul to arrive with his parents shortly after 6:00. He had to work today, so if they don't hit much traffic, we should be ready for dinner by 6:30." Catherine gave Sierra a compassionate smile. "I could show you to the guest room where Tawni and you will be staying, if you would like to rest a bit or maybe freshen up." She said it so nicely that Sierra decided she really liked Paul's grandmother. After hearing about his grandmother on his father's side, who lived in Scotland and rationed the heat when Paul had stayed with her on the weekends, Sierra found it hard to picture this elegant yet friendly and gracious woman as his other grandmother.

Sierra accepted the invitation to go to the guest room. As soon as Catherine closed the door, Sierra made a beeline to the adjacent bathroom, where she examined her eye. It was a lulu, no doubt about it. She was going to have to brace herself for all the "Rocky" jokes because there was no hiding this one.

Tawni's things were already unpacked in the room. Sierra wondered if her sister would mind if she borrowed a clean shirt. Certainly Tawni would understand when she saw the damage. She knew how deeply Sierra cared for

Paul. Tawni would want to do everything she could to aid Sierra in a successful reunion, wouldn't she?

Sierra's judgment instructed her not to touch any of her sister's things. Noticing the alarm clock on the dresser, Sierra saw it was only 3:30. Paul wouldn't be there for two hours. Maybe the best thing would be to stretch out on that inviting bed and let the ice pack work on the swelling. When Tawni arrived, Sierra would ask about a shirt or persuade Tawni to have their dad open the trailer for the luggage. Things were looking up. Maybe Sierra's reunion with Paul wouldn't be a disaster after all.

Stretching out on the queen-size bed, Sierra felt as if she could fall asleep then and there, it was so comfortable. Not a single lumpy duffel bag touched her anywhere. Within a few minutes, she did fall into a luxuriously deep sleep.

Tawni woke her some time later by gently shaking Sierra's shoulder and asking in a louder than normal voice the silliest question in the world, "Are you asleep?"

"I was," Sierra mumbled, forcing her eyes to open and trying to figure out where she was. Her left eye wouldn't open all the way. That's when she remembered.

"Did you lose this?" Tawni asked, holding up the defrosted bag of peas, which had fallen onto the floor.

"Ouch," Sierra said, sitting up.

"I guess," Tawni said, leaning closer for a more thorough examination of the swollen eye. "Why do these things always happen to you, Sierra?"

"Don't start with me, Tawni. I'm in a bad mood."

Tawni reared back and put her hand on her hip. She was a beautiful woman, even when she was putting on a mock show of being offended. Her year of working as a professional model had given her natural loveliness and grace added polish. She had tried out a variety of looks over the past year, including a wild array of hair colors. Today she looked more like her childhood self: Her hair was a soft strawberry blonde color, and she wore little makeup. She was still gorgeous, and once again Sierra felt the familiar stab of pain at being the little sister in the shadow of the perfect Tawni. The black eye only added to the tomboy memories from childhood. She felt more like a fifth-grader than a high school graduate who was moving into her dorm room next week.

"You don't have to leave it like that, you know," Tawni said, her voice soft but still carrying an edge to it. "Take a shower, and I'll put some makeup on it for you. I also have a few techniques to help with the swelling."

"I don't have any clean clothes."

"You can wear whatever you want of mine," Tawni offered.

Sierra hesitated only a moment before complying with her sister's directions. "Are Mom and Granna Mae here?" she asked.

"Yes. Granna Mae is taking a nap. Paul and his parents should be here in less than an hour, so you had better hurry."

Prompted by her sister's reality check, Sierra picked up the pace. Just before she closed the bathroom door, she turned and gave her sister a grateful smile, which also made her eye hurt. "Hey, Tawni, thanks. And congratulations on your engagement and everything."

Tawni's smile broadcast that she was a woman in love and nothing could ruin her mood, not even her kid sister with a black eye.

chapter five

SIERRA HURRIEDLY SHOWERED. SHE WAS BEGINNING TO feel anxious about seeing Paul. Tawni was nice to offer to give Sierra a speedy makeover for the event. Stepping back into the bedroom with the towel around her, Sierra spotted her mom sitting on the edge of the bed.

"Hi!" Sierra said, her mood definitely improving. "How was your trip down?"

Mrs. Jensen looked closely at Sierra. "Obviously a lot less eventful than yours. Gavin told me what happened. I'm so sorry, honey. He said you told him not to feel bad about it. I appreciate your saying that to him."

"It was an accident," Sierra said, adjusting her towel and wishing she had a robe to put on. It was much cooler in the bedroom than the bathroom, and she was getting goose bumps on her arms.

"I'm going to work a wonder on her," Tawni said, swishing past Sierra and carrying a large makeup case into the bathroom. "Let's decide what you're going to wear first because that might determine the hues I select."

"The hues?" Sierra questioned, giving her mom a silly grin. "Is that model talk for color?"

"Of course," Tawni said, making her way back into the

bedroom with quick yet fluid motions. She reached into
the closet and pulled out a short summer dress on a hanger
and gave it a snap in the air to chase away any wrinkles.
"What about this one?"

"For me?" Sierra skeptically scanned the short, thin,
straight dress. It was an earthy bronze color with embroi-
dery in matching thread around the scoop neck. This was
definitely a departure from the usual long, gauze skirts
Sierra picked up at the vintage thrift stores in Portland.
Tawni's selection had a Southwest, hot-summer-in-Ari-
zona look about it and was nothing Sierra would ever have
been drawn to in a store window.

"It might be a little short on Sierra," Mrs. Jensen said.

Suddenly, Sierra didn't think it was so short. Tawni was
taller than Sierra, and if Tawni could wear this dress, why
couldn't Sierra? Besides, they were in Southern California
now, and it was definitely hot. The dress would make her
look much older, and since Paul was two years older than
Sierra and had, in the past, alluded to her need to grow
up, this dress might just be the right item to wear. With a
little help from Tawni and her wardrobe, Sierra decided
she could grow up in the next half hour.

"I like it," Sierra said decidedly. "I'll put it on."

"Oh, no," Tawni said, pulling back the dress. "First the
makeup. Here, you can wear this robe, if you want. Start
drying your hair, but be sure to leave my diffuser on the
dryer. I don't want you to blow all the curl out."

Sierra gave her mom another comical expression and
then said, "Right, like that would ever happen. The curse
of the curls is with me for life, dear Tawni. As if you had
never noticed."

"Don't worry," Tawni said, with another vivacious grin. "I have plans for all those curls."

"Well," Mrs. Jensen said, rising from the bed. "I'm not sure I should stick around for this. It's hard on this old heart of mine to watch both of you turn into such lovely women before my eyes."

"You're just not used to seeing us get along so well," Sierra said. "It's the new, improved Tawni-and-Sierra relationship."

Mrs. Jensen stood another moment admiring her daughters before leaving the room. Her parting words were "I love you both."

"Here," Tawni said, handing Sierra a bottle of hair spritz. "Spray this on before you start drying. It'll protect your hair from the heat. And hurry."

"I'm hurrying, I'm hurrying." Sierra slipped into the bathroom, put on the robe, squirted the fine mist all over her hair, and went to work drying it. Tawni came in and began doing Sierra's makeup. Sierra gave up trying to dry her hair, since Tawni kept complaining that the air was blowing on her face.

Sitting as still as she could, Sierra allowed her sister to work her miracle. Tawni worked quickly and expertly, giving Sierra compliments along the way.

"You have the perfect shape of lips, you know. I wish mine were like that on top. I have to draw in the heart shape. And your skin is really clear. Have you been using anything special?"

"No."

"I always get blemishes right here on my chin. It doesn't look like you do."

"I get them behind my ears."

"At least you can hide those." Tawni stepped back and admired her work around Sierra's swollen eye. "Take a look."

Tawni moved away from the mirror, and Sierra was startled by her reflection. She looked stunning. The blackness had disappeared, and even the swelling had seemed to go down after Tawni applied a clear cream under her eye. The amount of makeup was more than Sierra had ever worn. Her blue-gray eyes were emphasized dramatically, and her lips were colored and looked ready for kissing.

"I look . . ." Sierra couldn't find the word.

"You look gorgeous," Tawni said. "Here, blot your lips. I know it's more than you would normally wear, but to get it all to blend with the color under your eyes, I had to go heavier. I think you look stunning, and Paul will be stunned when he sees you."

"You sure?"

Tawni nodded and checked her watch. "Oh no! We're running out of time. Let me get your hair up, and then you can dress. I have a pair of sandals that match the dress perfectly. You have shaved your legs recently, haven't you?"

Sierra quickly ran her fingers up her right leg. "They're not too bad."

"Honestly, Sierra. I shave my legs every time I take a shower. I've never understood how you could stand to have prickly legs."

"They're not prickly."

Tawni quickly ran her finger up Sierra's leg, taking her own test. "They're prickly. But that's the least of your concerns right now. First the hair, then the dress."

Eight minutes later, Sierra stood before the bathroom mirror trying to decide what she thought of her reflection.

Tawni had arranged Sierra's wild blonde curls on the top of her head by scooping them all up in a hair tie then letting the curls bubble out the top. With a dozen bobby pins, Tawni had twisted the larger curls and pinned them to the side of Sierra's head. She had a magazine in front of her the whole time with a picture of this style and told Sierra that when she first saw the picture she wanted to try fixing Sierra's hair that way.

Sierra had to admit the effect was dramatic, which meant the fancy hair went with the heavy makeup and the short dress. It all went together. And it wasn't too much, really. Tawni dressed like this all the time. It just didn't feel familiar, and that made it a little scary.

For a moment Sierra considered telling Tawni she couldn't go through with it. She couldn't meet Paul's parents for the first time looking like a junior Tawni model. And she couldn't meet Paul looking so different from when he had seen her last, more than a year ago. Could she? But then she thought of how this was Tawni's weekend, this was Tawni's party, and Tawni had had so much fun fixing Sierra up like this. It would certainly put her sister in a bad mood if Sierra rejected the makeover. She felt stuck.

With one more glance in the mirror, Sierra convinced herself she looked good. And she did look good. Stunning, actually. No one would disagree with that. Maybe stunning was a good thing for one night. One special night.

"Do you think they're here yet?" Sierra asked.

"No. I asked Jeremy to knock on the door when they arrived."

"Do you have your ring yet?" Sierra looked at her sister's hand and realized she should have asked this question an hour ago.

"No." Tawni held up her unadorned left hand. "Jeremy is going to give it to me tonight, I think. We picked it out, but it had to be sized."

Just then a knock sounded at the bedroom door. Tawni and Sierra spontaneously reached for each other and squeezed each other's arms. They had good reason to be a little excited and nervous. Those MacKenzie boys were the kind who took a girl's breath away.

"Yes?" Tawni called out.

"It's me." Jeremy's voice sounded through the closed door. "Just wanted to let you know my parents are here."

"Thanks. We'll be right out." Tawni checked her hair in the mirror and touched up her lipstick. The summer dress she wore was a pale tangerine and looked much more sophisticated than the "Arizona summer" outfit Sierra had wiggled into. Tawni's sandals had much lower heels than the ones Sierra had borrowed from her sister, so for one of the first times in their lives, the two sisters stood nearly eye level with each other.

"You look ravishing, as always," Sierra said.

Tawni flashed her a smile. "So do you. Come on. Let's face the cameras."

Sierra assumed that was some kind of model talk. She should have joined in the spirit of the comment when Tawni put her arm through Sierra's and led her from the guest room. She should have felt ravishing and confident. Instead of her tomboy cutoff jeans, her unruly hair flying every which way, and of course, the hideous black eye, she was dressed like a model and was a fitting counterpart for her sister. She should have been smiling for the cameras.

Yet all she could think as they exited the room was, *I'm about to make one of the worst mistakes of my life!*

chapter six

*J*EREMY'S COMMENT WHEN THE TWO SISTERS ENTERED the living room should have been reason enough for Sierra to take flight back to the guest room and conduct a little makeover of her own. Actually, it wasn't his comment so much as his expression. He said, "Sierra, is that you?" And he said it not as though he was impressed, but more as if he was amused. The tone was condescending, like an older brother discovering a younger sibling who has helped herself to Mommy's perfume and makeup.

"Doesn't she look terrific?" Tawni asked, going to Jeremy's side, slipping her hand into his, and standing back to admire her handiwork.

Sierra nervously fingered the silver daffodil necklace. Tawni had tried to convince Sierra that it didn't go with the outfit and she should tuck it under her dress, but Sierra wanted to wear it proudly so Paul would see how much she treasured his gift.

"Ah, yes," Jeremy said after a pause. "Terrific. I hardly knew it was you, Sierra."

Mr. Jensen walked in then with Wesley and Mrs. Jensen. They all had a stilted nod for her after hiding the surprised looks on their faces.

"You did a good job of covering up the shiner," Sierra's dad said graciously.

"What do you think of her hair? I got the style out of one of my bridal magazines. I wanted to try it out. It might be kind of cute for all the bridesmaids to wear their hair that way, don't you think?"

Sierra swallowed, waiting for all the Lookie Lous of her family to finish staring. She definitely wasn't cut out to be Tawni's guinea pig. In that moment Sierra decided she couldn't go through with this.

"You know what? I have a headache from my hair being coiled on top of my head like this. No offense, Tawni, but I'm going to take it down."

"Oh. Are you sure the headache is from your hair? Maybe it's from your eye. You could try some aspirin first, couldn't you?" Tawni looked heartbroken, but Sierra felt certain, as she heard voices approaching up the front walkway, that some things in life were more important than Tawni's feelings. A good impression with Paul and his family headed the top of Sierra's list at the moment.

"I'll take some," Sierra said, quickly turning to dash for the guest room, which was situated on the other side of the entryway. She was too late. Just as her sandaled foot hit the tiled entry, the front door opened, and a rush of voices overwhelmed her. Sierra tried to duck out of the way, but a large, friendly woman with brunette hair took her wrist and said, "Sierra? Are you Sierra?"

Sierra timidly nodded and could feel her pinned curls bob on top of her head. She didn't dare look behind the woman in case Paul was standing there.

"Sierra dear, you don't know how long I've waited to give you this!" And with that, the woman, who smelled of honeysuckle, wrapped her arms around Sierra and gave her about the biggest hug she had ever received. When the woman pulled away, she looked Sierra in the face and said, "I'm Lindy. Lindy MacKenzie. Paul's mom. And you're the little angel who prayed my boy back to us." She scooped up Sierra's hands in hers and held them tightly. "You'll never know how much I cherish you, sweet Sierra." Tears were in her eyes. "And I understand we even share the same birthday—November 14th."

Suddenly, Sierra knew her outward appearance didn't matter to this woman. Lindy MacKenzie saw straight to the inside of people and embraced them heart to heart. Sierra felt at ease, and not ridiculous, in her fancy hairdo and tight dress. Paul's mother had showered her with the happy scent of honeysuckle, and Sierra knew somehow she could face whatever the rest of this weekend might hold.

Mrs. MacKenzie gave Sierra's hands another good squeeze, and with a twinkle in her eye, she said, "I'd like you to meet my first husband, Robert."

"First husband?" Sierra questioned as she reached out her hand to shake with Pastor MacKenzie. He was a calm, gentle man who had lots of dark, wavy hair like Paul and wore small, wire-rim glasses.

"Lindy likes to call me that to see people's reactions," Pastor MacKenzie said with a wink at Sierra. "I also happen to be her only husband."

Sierra got the joke, as silly as it was, and nodded her understanding to Pastor MacKenzie.

Mrs. MacKenzie jumped in with another story. "An older woman from the congregation of our last church lived in a retirement community, and you'll never guess what she did. This is a true story. She went up to one of the gentlemen who lived there and said, 'You look just like my third husband.' And the gentleman said, 'Third husband? How many have you had?' And she said to him, 'Only two . . . so far.' And would you believe, they were married the next month? Robert performed the ceremony."

Lindy MacKenzie filled the room with her cheerful chuckle, and Sierra decided she had never met a woman like her. Sierra adored her.

Mr. Jensen stepped into the entryway and said, "That's some pickup line. How are you, Robert? Good to see you again, Lindy."

Sierra glanced over Pastor MacKenzie's shoulder to see if Paul was standing on the front door step next to the clay pot with the tiny blue flowers spilling over the sides. She saw only Dillon bending down to pet a large calico cat, and she could hear Gavin calling to him from around the side of the house. Unconsciously biting her lower lip, Sierra wondered if she should venture outside in hopes of finding Paul so the two of them could share a private reunion. Of course, either of her little brothers might bombard her with a bunch of immature comments about her appearance, and that was the last thing she needed in front of Paul—especially since Mrs. MacKenzie had managed to lift her spirits in such a way that Sierra's attention was off herself.

Pastor MacKenzie closed the front door behind him and headed for the living room.

"Is Paul still coming?" Sierra asked in a voice that sounded much too squeaky.

"He's here already," Pastor MacKenzie said. "He drove up himself after work so he could have his car here. It was in the driveway when we arrived. He must be out back."

Now Sierra felt nervous all over again. She had to figure out a way to casually wander through this chattering crowd in the entryway and living room and figure out how to get to the backyard. Slipping around the giddy relatives, Sierra tried the hallway that contained her guest room. She passed a bathroom, two closed doors, and then entered a large kitchen and dining area with huge windows that faced the ocean. The view was spectacular. A wide patio stretched out behind the house and was met by a carpet of deep grass. To the left, on the grass, was a small white gazebo, and next to it was a trail that appeared to lead down to the beach.

Sierra leaned up against the counter by the sink, hoping to be hidden just a little as she scanned the backyard for Paul. Dillon was running with a croquet mallet in his hand and yelling for Gavin to come back and finish the game with him. She saw no sign of Paul. But the view captivated Sierra, and she watched the white, soaring seagulls as they circled in the pale blue sky.

As she stared out the window, someone quietly entered the kitchen behind her and said, "Excuse me. Do you know what time my grandmother is planning to have dinner?"

Sierra couldn't move. She knew that deep male voice. She would know it anywhere. Ever since the first time that voice spoke to her at the phone booth in London and said, "Excuse me, but do you have any coins? I'm desperate!" she had known that voice. But now she couldn't respond.

"Oh, ah," Paul said to the back of Sierra's head. "*¿Qué tiempo esta noche es la comida?*"

Sierra nearly burst out laughing. Paul apparently thought she was a maid his grandmother had hired to help with all the company. Slowly turning to him, with a straight face, she answered in her equally broken Spanish, "*Yo no sé, Señor.*"

Paul gave her the strangest look.

Sierra tried hard not to crack up. He kept staring at her until the corners of her mouth finally pulled themselves up in a huge grin, and she said, "*Hola*, Paul."

"Sierra?" It was barely a whisper. Then again he said, "Sierra!" as if he finally did recognize her through the makeup and hair and imperfect Spanish accent. Now it was his turn to start laughing.

Sierra's big plans for their romantic reunion turned into the kind of story Mrs. MacKenzie might tell at a church social. There Paul and Sierra stood, four feet from each other in the middle of the kitchen, both laughing their hearts out, but neither of them moving toward the other. Theirs was a nervous, relieved, caught-in-the-act kind of laugh. It helped Sierra to realize Paul must be feeling all the same crazy things she was feeling.

The first wave of laughter subsided, and Sierra caught her breath. She inched closer to him, moving awkwardly in the high-heeled sandals across the slick kitchen floor. Paul didn't move, though. He stayed still, staring at her with a strange look on his face, as if he couldn't quite figure out if she really was Sierra or if this was some kind of bizarre joke.

"It's really me," Sierra heard herself say, shrugging her shoulders and feeling her heart beating all the way up into her throat.

Paul was wearing a white cotton shirt with the sleeves rolled up, khaki shorts, and a pair of sandals with dark straps. His brown, wavy hair was cut short and combed back on the sides. A few rebellious strands curved at his right temple, and across his broad forehead were hints of thin worry lines. His stormy, blue-gray eyes met hers and stayed locked on her for an unblinking moment.

"Hi," he finally said.

Unsure of what to do or say, Sierra swallowed her disappointment over this not being the fairy-tale reunion she had planned. She found her shaky voice and whispered back, "Hi."

chapter seven

"OH, GOOD!" LINDY MACKENZIE DECLARED, making a grand entrance into the kitchen. "There you two are. So you've found each other. Isn't this wonderful? I've been looking forward to this get-together more than I can tell you." She stepped over to Sierra's side and gave her a quick, around-the-shoulder hug. "How about something to drink for you two? I see a pitcher of lemonade there on the table. Would either of you like some?"

Sierra couldn't answer. She didn't want lemonade. She wanted Paul's arm around her instead of his mother's. And she wanted him to stop staring at her and to smile. Really smile. Smile the unspoken message that he had been looking forward to this get-together more than his mom had and that he was happy to see Sierra.

Before either of them could answer, the group from the living room had made its way into the kitchen, and with the crowd came noise and confusion. Sierra was instructed by her mother to wake up Granna Mae from her nap. Lindy announced that they weren't eating at the house, as Paul had supposed. They were going out to dinner and planned to leave in five minutes.

Sierra turned away from her mom, preparing to head back to the hallway, which meant she had to walk past Paul. Maybe he would duck out with her, and they could have their hug in the hallway. But when she turned, Paul had disappeared.

She strode to the hallway, hoping he was already there waiting for her, but the hall was empty. Sierra tapped on the first closed door and called out for Granna Mae. When Sierra heard no answer, she opened the door and tapped again lightly. Granna Mae was asleep on top of a blue and white floral bedspread with a thin blanket over her legs. Her soft, white hair billowed between her head and the pillow, making it look as if she were sleeping on a cloud. Her wrinkled face wore a blissful expression.

Leaning over, Sierra touched her grandmother's shoulder and whispered, "Granna Mae, time to wake up."

Granna Mae's eyelids fluttered open. The instant she looked at Sierra, Sierra knew her sometimes-confused grandmother didn't recognize her. A cloudy look was in Granna Mae's eyes, and her blissful expression had turned into irritation. "What?" the old woman said impatiently.

"Granna Mae, we're at Tawni's engagement party, and we're all going to go out to eat for dinner now. Are you ready to wake up so you can come with us?"

"What?"

Sierra repeated the information more slowly and then gently coaxed her grandmother to get up. "That's good," Sierra said as Granna Mae swung her legs over the side of the bed. "You'll feel better once you've had some dinner."

"I'm not sick," Granna Mae snapped.

"I know you're not sick. It's just that it's dinnertime, and we're all going to a restaurant now." Sierra realized she looked different to Granna Mae, since she had never dressed up like this before; the transformation could have been confusing even to someone who didn't have memory lapses. Sierra's appearance certainly hadn't impressed Paul.

Sierra held out her hand. After scrutinizing her for another moment, Granna Mae hesitantly took her hand and allowed Sierra to lead her out of the bedroom.

Mrs. Jensen met them in the hallway and gave Sierra a raised-eyebrow look that Sierra knew meant, "How's she doing? Is she coherent?"

Sierra shook her head and lowered her eyes, letting her mother know that this was not one of Granna Mae's clearer moments. When Granna Mae was thinking clearly, she would call Sierra by her childhood nickname, "Lovey." For some reason, Sierra was the family member Granna Mae recognized most often in her fuzzy spells, which was why Mrs. Jensen had sent Sierra in to wake up her grandmother.

"We're going in Jeremy's car," Mrs. Jensen said to Granna Mae. "We're all going out to a Mexican restaurant for dinner."

Granna Mae looked at Sierra and then at her mother. "I don't know anyone named Jeremy. Where's Paul?"

Mrs. Jensen and Sierra snapped a glance of surprise at each other. Sierra was the first to respond. "Paul is here. He'll be glad to see you, too."

Sierra had no way of knowing if Granna Mae truly meant Paul MacKenzie or if she was referring to her son Paul, who had been killed in Vietnam. Granna Mae had met Paul MacKenzie when she was in the hospital more than a year ago. Paul had paid her an unannounced visit and brought her a daffodil, which Granna Mae declared was her favorite flower. It was the same day Paul had seen

Sierra parading down the street with her armful of daffodils, and he had dubbed her "Daffodil Queen" shortly after
that in his first letter.

They stepped into the crowded entryway, and Sierra
could tell all the loud voices were frightening Granna Mae.
She looked at the group as if she didn't know anyone, not
even her own son Howard, who was Sierra's dad. Granna
Mae clutched Sierra's hand tighter, and together they
maneuvered through the group and out the front door. As
soon as they were outside, Granna Mae seemed to start
breathing again, and she loosened her grip on Sierra's
hand. Sierra was amazed at how soft her grandmother's
hand felt even though the skin was sagging around her
bony fingers and wrist.

"Mom said you're going to ride in Jeremy's car," Sierra
said slowly, leading Granna Mae to the driveway, where all
the cars were packed in, bumper to bumper. "You and
Mom will ride to the restaurant with Jeremy and Tawni."

"And you," Granna Mae said, quickly tightening up on
Sierra's hand.

Sierra didn't know how to tell her grandmother that
Sierra's secret plan was to go in Paul's car—just she and
Paul, alone at last so they could talk. She hadn't spotted
Paul since he had disappeared from the kitchen, but she
had thought through the seating arrangements in the car,
as well as when they arrived at the restaurant. Her plan
was to put herself next to Paul the whole time—not next
to Granna Mae.

"Well, Mom will be with you," Sierra said. The others
were following Sierra and Granna Mae out to the driveway,
and Sierra expected to turn around and see Paul any second.

Granna Mae held tightly to Sierra's hand and looked confused.

"My mom," Sierra explained slowly. "My mom, Sharon Jensen, will be with you in the car."

"Sharon?"

"Yes. You know, she married your son Howard."

"Oh." Then after a pause, Granna Mae said, "Is this their wedding party?"

"No. It's Tawni's engagement party. Tawni and Jeremy. We're going out to eat with Jeremy's family and our family."

Granna Mae looked up at the crowd that was now gathered in the driveway. Sierra knew they were all watching her with her grandmother and waiting to take a cue from her as to what to do next.

"Would you like to ride in the backseat?" Sierra asked.

Suddenly, Granna Mae let go of Sierra's hand and held both her arms out to the group of relatives. "Paul dear," she said cheerfully. "Oh, Paul, how wonderful to see you."

Sierra looked at the surprised group and watched as Paul moved around from the rear flank next to his father and came toward Granna Mae with his arms open to her. Paul was reaching with open arms for her grandmother, when all along Sierra had planned for him to run to *her* with open arms. He hugged Granna Mae gently, and as Sierra watched from less than a foot away, Paul tenderly pressed his lips against Granna Mae's soft cheek and gave her a kiss.

Granna Mae gave no indication if she knew he was Paul MacKenzie or if she thought he was her son. Sierra admired Paul all the more when he spoke to Granna Mae. He knew she might be confused about who he was, but that didn't matter to him. He treated her with dignity and tenderness.

"Would you like to ride to the restaurant with me?" Paul asked Granna Mae, bending down so he could look her in the eyes.

"Oh, yes. I'd love to go with you and Becky."

Paul shot a questioning look at Sierra. She gestured that she had no idea who Becky was.

Sierra's mom stepped forward. "That's a great idea, Granna Mae. Why don't we all go in Paul's car?" Mrs. Jensen took Sierra by the elbow and urged her into the backseat of the dark blue sedan while Paul helped Granna Mae into the front seat. Mrs. Jensen leaned over and whispered to Sierra, "Becky was Paul's fiancée. They got engaged the week before he left for Vietnam. You've probably met her. She married Mrs. Kraus's son."

Sierra shook her head. She didn't remember any daughter-in-law of Mrs. Kraus's named Becky ever coming into the bakery. It was all too strange—too connected. It reminded Sierra, as she had noted in the past, that everyone is so connected it's a good idea not to alienate or offend others. Right now Paul was doing an exceptionally good job of honoring Granna Mae and helping Sierra and her mom make this a comfortable situation for both families. Sierra's heightened opinion of Paul almost made up for their reunion being awkward. Almost, but not quite.

As they drove through the beach town's narrow streets, Sierra considered what maneuvers might be necessary for her to sit next to Paul at the restaurant. If she could make those arrangements, she felt certain she and Paul could relate on a more comfortable level. All the letters they had exchanged for the past year and the phone conversations in which they had laughed together late at night had led Sierra to believe they were very close—boyfriend-and-girlfriend close, even though they had never used those terms nor had they ever defined their relationship. The only part that had been missing over this year had been the physical contact. Sierra felt certain that if they could just break that barrier, their relationship would move forward.

By the time they pulled into the parking lot of the large Mexican restaurant, Sierra had dreamed up a lovely plan. She would sit next to Paul, nice and close; and without anyone else knowing it, they would hold hands under the table. Her plan was to be close enough and her hand accessible enough that Paul would know instinctively to take it. That way he would be making the first move—sort of. She also had a backup plan. If he didn't take her hand, she would slip her fingers over his, and then he could decide what position their holding hands should take, and they could adjust.

It seemed perfect. Of course, being inexperienced at these things, Sierra was a little unsure of how it would all actually happen. The most important thing to her was that it would be natural. The memory of it would be wonderfully sweet and would help erase the memory of their silly encounter in the kitchen.

But none of her careful planning included Granna Mae's unpredictable actions and her selective memory.

chapter eight

EFORE SIERRA HAD STEPPED THREE FEET AWAY from Paul's car, Granna Mae reached for Sierra's hand and held it tightly. Her grandmother smiled happily and appeared coherent. Then she reached out her hand to Paul, inviting him to take her other hand. While Mrs. Jensen waited for the others to arrive, Granna Mae, Paul, and Sierra walked hand in hand through the parking lot and into the restaurant.

Sierra tried to steal a glance at Paul to see how he was reacting to this. He was studying his sandals as he walked and seemed unaware of Sierra's glances.

They entered the restaurant, and Granna Mae proudly announced to the hostess and several people waiting to be seated, "They're getting married!" She held up her arms so that Sierra and Paul's hands were raised as if in triumph.

"Congratulations," the hostess said.

"We're, um . . ." Paul hesitated. He glanced at Granna Mae and then flashed a quick look at Sierra. "We're here for the MacKenzie party. I believe we have the back room reserved."

"Oh, yes. For the engagement party. Congratulations again."

Paul nodded his thanks, playing along for Granna Mae's sake. Sierra noticed his neck had turned red. His face was turned away from her, but Granna Mae still had a lock grip on both their hands.

Sierra wanted to burst out laughing again. She knew if she did, it would take the tension out of this crazy situation and help Paul relax. But an outburst of Sierra's wild, pent-up laughter would probably upset her grandmother. Opting for Granna Mae's stability, Sierra swallowed her nervous laughter and prayed that Granna Mae wouldn't make another announcement to the Jensen and MacKenzie families, which had now entered the restaurant.

As hard as she tried, Sierra couldn't get Granna Mae to let go of her hand. The way they were headed, Granna Mae would be sitting between her and Paul the entire dinner. Sierra panicked at the thought.

Like a bad plot in a TV sitcom, Sierra's worst predictions came true. Granna Mae did sit between Paul and her. The speaker above Sierra's head played loud mariachi music throughout the whole meal. Everyone else was so busy chatting that no one noticed that Granna Mae kept holding Sierra's hand under the table, as if she were insecure and couldn't bring herself to let go.

Sierra tried to remind herself that this party was for Tawni. It was her engagement, her time to shine. And she did so—beautifully. Every now and then Tawni and Jeremy exchanged tender looks. Twice he kissed her on the cheek, and once she burst out laughing at something he said. Her laugh was wonderfully melodic, the kind Sierra had heard only a few times from her sister. Sierra knew Tawni was happy—deliriously happy—and that was supposed to matter the most.

However, Sierra was experiencing a desperate, sinking feeling—a deep sadness because none of her dreams was coming true. She had waited so long to see Paul, to be with him. And now nothing was going the way she had hoped.

Why isn't Paul trying to talk to me? she thought as she picked at her meal. *He could have found a way to sit next to me if he had wanted to. Maybe he doesn't want to. Maybe the feelings I have for him don't match any he has for me. Maybe this is all a huge mistake, a big joke, and I'm the punch line.*

Sierra's head hurt. She knew it was partly due to the impractical hairstyle. With all her heart she wished she could go back to the house, change out of her tight dress that was becoming uncomfortable to sit in, wash the sticky makeup off her face, and release her curls from their fashion prison. Then she would find her way down the trail by the gazebo, dig her bare feet into the sand, and let the gentle Pacific waves tickle her toes.

The evening dragged on as each of the fathers stood to say something wonderful about their children. Tomorrow afternoon a big engagement reception would be held at the church in San Diego where Paul and Jeremy's dad was the pastor. Tonight was just for family, and so the speeches were personal.

Both fathers pledged their wholehearted support to Jeremy as he took this next step into manhood. Sierra's dad invited Jeremy to come to him at any time if he needed anything, and then he charged Jeremy to take his responsibilities to Tawni seriously as he now made public his pledge to marry her. Pastor MacKenzie then stood and read a verse from Ephesians about Christians being Christ's bride and how Christ gave Himself for her. Jeremy's father

talked about the Hebrew tradition in which the bride-
groom would declare publicly his love for and commitment to his bride and then go to prepare a place for them
to live.

"This is a beautiful picture of what Christ has done for
us," Pastor MacKenzie said, his deep voice booming over
the piped-in mariachi music. "Christ came to earth to
declare His undying love for us. He even called us His
bride. Then He returned to His Father's house to prepare
a place for us. One day soon He'll come back for us and
take us to be with Him forever. Until that day, Christ has
left the Holy Spirit with us as evidence of His commitment
to those who believe in Him. The Holy Spirit is God's
engagement ring around our lives, His promise that we
will one day be united with Him."

Sierra felt a rush of goose bumps stream up her arms.
She had never seen the parallel before. Being a Christian
meant she was, in a sense, spiritually engaged to the Lord.
He loved her and wanted her to be with Him forever. The
truth burrowed itself in her heart.

Pastor MacKenzie sat down, and Jeremy stood. He
looked a little nervous but determined. In his hand he held
a small black box. Turning to face a radiant Tawni, he said,
"I now want to make a promise to you, Tawni. This ring
is a symbol of my commitment to you and evidence to
others of my love for you. In giving it to you, I'm asking
that you will save yourself for me alone and that one day
soon you'll marry me and spend the rest of your life with
me."

Tears clouded Sierra's eyes. She saw the twins of her
own tears running down her sister's cheeks as Tawni stood
and gracefully held out her hand to Jeremy. "I accept this

ring with all my heart, Jeremy. And yes, I promise to marry you."

Sierra could hear sniffs all around the table as the women and some of the men tried to keep back their tears. Sierra noticed that, miraculously, the annoying music had stopped, and the room was silent as the family watched Jeremy take the ring from the box and slip it on Tawni's finger. The newly committed couple tenderly, comfortably, kissed each other.

Enthusiastic applause burst from around the long table, and as if on cue, the music cranked up again, with trumpets blaring right above Sierra's head. She clapped and wished her oldest brother, Cody, could have been there. He and his wife, Katrina, recently had had a baby girl, and she had been sick with an ear infection, which made it unwise to travel, since she was so young. If Cody and Katrina had been there, then it would have really felt as if the whole Jensen family were entering into this engagement with Tawni. A MacKenzie family member was missing, too. Paul and Jeremy also had an older brother who wasn't able to join them, although Sierra never heard exactly why.

Tawni sat down and admired the sparkling diamond ring on her finger. Her smile was electric, and Sierra was sure she had never seen her sister happier.

Wiping away her tears with a napkin, Sierra noticed she left a streak of foundation on the white cloth. She had wanted to look past Granna Mae over at Paul to see how he was reacting to all this, but the realization that her tears had probably made a mess of Tawni's makeup job prompted Sierra to quietly excuse herself and make an exit for the rest room.

One glance in the mirror and Sierra knew she couldn't

take the hairdo or the heavy makeup another minute. It wasn't that she looked bad or overdone by the standards of most magazines. Tawni had done an expert job, and the mascara must have been smudge-proof because no evidence showed of its smearing. Sierra just didn't look like herself. And that bothered her.

She was about to start pulling out the bobby pins when the door to the rest room opened and her mom stepped in.

"Are you all right?" she asked Sierra.

"Yes. I thought I'd smeared this makeup all over my face when I started to cry. Wasn't that beautiful—what the dads said and when Jeremy gave her the ring?"

Mrs. Jensen nodded and smiled. "It was wonderful. I wanted to make sure you were okay, though."

Sierra nodded. "I'm tired of being Tawni's beauty makeover project. I want to wash my face and take down my hair."

"You had better wait," Mrs. Jensen said. "Everyone is ready to leave now. Catherine has dessert for us back at the house, and I think Granna Mae is about as confused as she's ever been."

"I know," Sierra said. "She thought Paul and I were announcing our engagement! She told the hostess and everyone in the waiting area that we were getting married."

"Oh dear," Mrs. Jensen said, biting her lower lip. Sierra never noticed it before, but her mother did that often. That had to be where Sierra picked up the habit. "I've noticed you and Paul haven't exactly said a lot to each other. Is everything okay between you?"

Before Sierra could answer, Paul's mom entered the bathroom and said, "There you two are. We're ready to go.

Paul and Jeremy have already left, so you can both come with me."

"What about Granna Mae?" Mrs. Jensen asked.

"She went with Paul. I don't think she was willing to let go of his arm for anything. It's kind of sweet the way she has taken to him."

Sierra followed her mom and Paul's mom to the parking lot and sat in the car's backseat. As soon as they reached the house, Sierra rushed to the guest room. She wriggled herself out of Tawni's bronze dress and slipped into her cutoff jeans. It felt wonderful to breathe again. Rummaging through Tawni's neatly organized clothes, Sierra found a sweatshirt and carried it into the bathroom.

She released her captive curls, scrubbed her face, and removed all the eye makeup. The face that returned her gaze a moment later was a much happier, less sophisticated, much cleaner face. The only problem was the shiner. It hadn't magically gone away while the makeup covered it.

Sierra considered trying to dab a little of Tawni's concealer back on the blackened area, but she wasn't sure it would work without all the other layers Tawni had applied. She pulled the sweatshirt over her head and shook out her tangled tresses before running a hair pick through them.

"This is the real me," Sierra declared to her reflection, as if she were preparing for what she would say to Paul when he saw the downsized version of her hair and face. "Take me for what I am or walk away now, buddy, because this is reality."

As soon as she said it, Sierra had a terrible thought. What if Paul did decide to walk away? What if all this reality was a little too much for him? And could she blame him? The guy had just spent a quiet year in the Scottish

Highlands, and here he was, with her wacky Granna Mae clinging to him and making false public announcements, and his brother and her sister entering into a sacred agreement. What if Paul did get a good look at the reality that was and would always be "Sierra Jensen"? What if she walked into that living room and this guy, who had captured her heart through his words written in bold, black letters on 100 sheets of onionskin paper, decided to walk away?

Time seemed to freeze.

"There's only one way to find out," Sierra finally told her reflection. "It's now or never."

chapter nine

WHEN SIERRA ENTERED THE LIVING ROOM, WEARing her own familiar sandals, her well-worn jeans shorts, and Tawni's sweatshirt, she found the room empty. All the voices seemed to be coming from the backyard.

Walking through the kitchen and out the back door, she found the group gathered around the patio table and sitting on the chaise lounges and cushioned patio chairs. Lindy MacKenzie was busy helping Gavin and Dillon scoop ice cream for themselves from the cartons set on the table. It appeared that dessert was a make-it-yourself ice cream sundae bar.

Sierra looked around for Paul. He wasn't there. Her heart started flip-flopping again. What if he had left? What if he already had done a reality check, and having fulfilled his duty as a good son and brother by attending the engagement dinner, he had taken off?

Before she could sink into a bog of despair, Paul's deep voice sounded from behind her. "This was the only one in the freezer in the garage." He placed a carton of vanilla ice cream on the table. "Do you want me to go to the store for some more chocolate ice cream?"

"No, this is fine. Just fine," his mom said. "I think we have plenty." When Lindy looked up at Paul, she noticed Sierra standing at the table with her back to him. Sierra hadn't quite gotten up the nerve to turn around and face him. The look on Mrs. MacKenzie's face showed that she was surprised by Sierra's transformation. Sierra saw a trace of a wince, too, which was probably directed at the black eye. Then Mrs. MacKenzie smiled just as she had when she first had hugged Sierra and said, "Did you get yourself a sundae yet, Sierra?"

"Not yet." She was thankful Mrs. MacKenzie hadn't made a big to-do about how different Sierra looked. She could almost feel Paul staring at the back of her head, willing her to turn around, but she kept her chin tucked and bit her lip.

"Me neither," Paul said. He stretched his arm past Sierra on her left side, reaching for a bowl. She felt his arm brush her shoulder. He picked up two bowls and held one out for Sierra. "Here you go," he said.

Sierra drew in a deep breath and slowly turned to face him. She hoped her sincere, fresh, clean smile would make up for the shock when he saw her like this, only inches away.

Paul didn't even flinch. He stared the way she remembered him staring at her on the plane when they first met. His hand went gently to the black circle under her eye, and he touched her cheek just to the side of the bruise, the way a child might touch a floating soap bubble in fascination.

"It was an accident," Sierra explained before Paul could ask. "In the car on the way here. A can of root beer."

Paul nodded slowly, sympathetically. He seemed to be

taking in her face and hair as if for the first time.

Sierra continued to whisper her explanations to Paul as if no one else were around. "Tawni wanted to fix me up for the dinner. I guess she thought the other hairstyle went with the makeup she used to cover my black eye."

Paul nodded again, this time with a smile on his lips. He took Sierra by the elbow and whispered one word in her ear: "Come."

It was all she could do not to drop the ceramic ice cream bowl on the patio. She managed to place it on the table, and although Paul had let go of her elbow, she felt he had an invisible hold on her as he led her past all the chattering guests and across the grass toward the gazebo. Without saying anything, Paul led the way to the trail and down the wooden steps to the beach. The farther away from their families they walked, the louder the pounding surf grew.

The sun was hidden behind a bank of thick clouds that seemed to ride the edge of the horizon like a great battle-ship. In only a few minutes the sun would surrender behind that hulk of a ship, and this day would be over. But Sierra felt sure that, for Paul and her, this day was just about to begin.

When she reached the last step, Sierra slipped off her sandals, just as Paul had done, and followed his lead. She tucked the sandals under the step for safekeeping until their walk brought them back this way.

Paul shuffled through the sand with Sierra beside him. She loved the way the brown-sugar grains felt between her toes, cool and soothing like millions of tiny massage balls on the bottom of her feet.

They strolled and watched the glow of the sun diminish. Side by side, step matching step, neither of them spoke. A salty breeze whipped Sierra's hair into her face. A sandpiper scurried after the receding waves, pecking the bubbles in the sand, hoping to find its dinner.

No words seemed to come to either Sierra or Paul. With so much to say, Sierra didn't know where to begin. She felt peaceful and yet wired at the same time. Finally, she couldn't stand it. "Wait!" she said. "Stand right there. Don't move."

Paul stopped and stood with his bare feet sinking into the wet sand. Sierra walked a few feet away and turned to face Paul. The wind was now in her face, and it blew her curls away from her eyes. Paul stood still as a wave came up and covered his feet, burying them deeper in the sand.

In the cool evening light, Sierra could see his peaceful expression. He looked happy enough without adding anything to this moment. Sierra was the one who needed something else.

"Okay," she said, hoping this wasn't going to look strange to Paul. "This is how I wanted it to be when we first saw each other." She smiled and held out her arms, delightfully crying out, "Paul! It's you! It's really you!"

Paul caught on to her game, and holding out his arms, he declared, "Sierra! After all these long months, we're finally together!"

The scene was silly and more melodramatic than any Sierra had rehearsed in her imagination, but the essence was still there. They could now run into each other's arms.

One problem, though. The surf had buried Paul's feet in the sand, and Sierra was the only one running. She hit Paul's chest with a thud and bashed the underside of her sore eye.

"Ouch!" she yelped, pulling away and doing a little circle-of-agony dance.

"Are you okay?" Paul released his feet and stepped to her side, gently touching her shoulder.

"I hit my eye on your chest. What have you been doing? Working out or something? It felt like a rock." For emphasis, she playfully swung at Paul's chest and hit something hard again.

"Careful," he said, pulling out a cassette tape in a plastic holder from his pocket. "This was supposed to be a present for you. I forgot I put it in that pocket." He held out the tape. "It's some Scottish music. Remember? I told you I'd buy you a tape."

"Oh, yeah. Thanks. I think." She still held her left hand over her sore eye. "Actually, why don't you keep it for me. I don't think it would fit in any of my pockets."

"Sure." Paul took the cassette back and tucked it into his shirt pocket with a pat. "Just remember it's there, and don't go crashing into it again."

Sierra slowly lowered her hand and tried her best to smile without making the muscles under her eye move upward. "Ouch," she said again. "It hurts too much to smile."

"You don't have to smile," Paul said. He was looking at her warmly, and she could tell he was content just to be with her.

After the endless hours of staring at the picture Paul had sent her, Sierra had thought she had his face memorized. But now she knew she didn't. The soft summer evening light, the way his hair was cut shorter than in the photo, and the gentle expression were all different from the image she had memorized of Paul MacKenzie. This was real. He was real. And he was here, only a few inches away from her.

"Take my hand," Sierra heard herself say. It was exactly what she had been thinking, but she hadn't planned to say it aloud.

"Yes, ma'am," Paul said with a laugh, responding playfully to her command. He reached for her hand, and she met his halfway and grasped it securely. Paul stopped laughing.

Wow! He felt that, too, Sierra thought with a thrill. *I know he did.*

Sierra's left arm had turned warm, as if low-wattage electricity had shot through it. She and her buddy Randy had held hands before, but she never had felt like this inside when they did.

"Let's walk," Paul suggested, still holding her hand firmly in his.

They walked silently for many minutes along the shoreline before loosening the grip they each had on the other. Sierra felt as if she had waited too many months for this experience to let go now. But their hands were getting sweaty, and Sierra felt a tiny muscle cramp in her thumb. The loosening of their grasp was a good thing. It relaxed their hands and arms and seemed to relax them as well.

"I wrote you a poem," Paul said, breaking their long silence.

"You did?"

"I wrote it last week when I was thinking about what it would be like when we finally saw each other again."

Sierra could feel her heart beating faster. She wondered if Paul had been looking forward to seeing her as much as she had been looking forward to seeing him. He must have if he wrote her a poem.

"Let's see if I can remember it." Paul led Sierra to where a cliff met the sand and a hollow had been dug out of the ancient rock by the high tide. He let go of her hand, and she settled herself into the cleft of the rock, out of the wind, where it was quieter and warmer and she could hear Paul's rich voice.

He looked into Sierra's eyes and began his poem:

"I asked you once
If you could fly;
You promised me
You had no wings.
Why did you lie?
How else
Could you have come
Across the sea
To my dark tower,
Bringing bread and light
To me?
I learned to know
The sound
Of stirring air,
Of candlelight,
And whispered prayer.
Can you tell me truly
You weren't there
Far across the sea?
Now distance
Is a walking space;
In full light I see your face.

But tell me,
Now
Where do you hide your wings?"

"Wow," was the only word that came to Sierra's lips. "Say it again," she urged him.

Paul repeated it and added for her interpretation, "I was thinking of how all we've had for so long were words between us. Words we wrote in letters and words we sent to heaven as we prayed for each other." Paul reached over and took Sierra's hand from where it rested in her lap. He laced his thick fingers in hers and said, "Or mostly your prayers for me, and then my returned prayers for you more recently."

Sierra affectionately gave Paul's hand a squeeze and added her interpretation to his poem. "And those words flew back and forth across the ocean and into the heavens for a year. Now we're close enough—what did you call it?—distance . . ."

"Distance is a walking space."

"Yes. A walking space and . . ."

Paul finished for her. "In full light I see your face."

Sierra felt herself blushing. A smile crept up her face, making her tender left eye hurt. "And let me guess," she said, pointing to her black eye. "This isn't exactly the face you expected to see."

"Actually," Paul said, tilting his head and looking at her closely enough to count every blessed freckle on her nose, "this is much more what I expected to see than what you surprised me with in the kitchen."

Sierra laughed. "Ow! That hurts." She tried to make her face go straight.

"Come here," Paul said tenderly. He let go of her hand and slid across the sand so that he was sitting next to her in the partial windbreak of their private little cove. He put his arm around her shoulder and invited her to rest her unbruised cheek against his shoulder.

Sierra felt herself relax as she snuggled up next to Paul. He smelled good. Not like the fresh evergreen scent of pine trees at Christmas when she had first met him. Now he smelled like pure soap and fresh laundered sheets that have hung on the line. His arm felt warm across her shoulders. His chin rested against the side of her head.

Together they sat close in the sand and watched the waves roll in and out. Neither of them said a word.

chapter ten

SIERRA LAY IN BED A LONG TIME THAT NIGHT, FINDING it impossible to fall asleep. Tawni, beside her in the guest bed was already sleeping when Sierra had tiptoed in well after midnight. Sierra had undressed for bed quietly and then lay there wishing her sister would wake up so Sierra could share the details of the evening with her. Especially because it had ended so confusingly.

Sierra coughed to see if that would disturb Tawni. It didn't. Then Sierra was glad it hadn't. She changed her mind about talking to Tawni. These details were hers alone; maybe she didn't want to share them with anyone. At least not until she had made some sense of them herself. She knew Amy and Vicki would never forgive her if she didn't provide them with an update before the weekend was over. She had a lot of fast figuring out to do.

Sierra turned over onto her back and stared at the tiny flecks of silver that glistened in the paint of the textured ceiling. The night-light in the bathroom gave the silver flecks their glow, but they were nothing compared with the glow of the stars Sierra and Paul had watched. The moon, wearing a half-grin, had looked down on them. And Sierra had worn a half-grin all evening, too. It hurt her face too much to smile, but it hurt her joyful heart too much not to smile.

For a wonderfully long time, Sierra and Paul had sat silently snuggling in their little cave. Then they rose and walked along the beach, hand in hand again. This time they didn't clasp hands so tightly. A settled peace had come over them, and they held hands playfully. First, with their fingers intertwined. Then, sometime later, when the conversation turned to Granna Mae and Sierra's appreciation for Paul's being so understanding, they linked only their first two fingers together and let their arms swing.

Sierra saw a shell and bent to pick it up. Paul teasingly pushed her toward the oncoming surf. She kept her balance and pulled herself up by his grasp. Then, using a self-defense technique Wesley had taught her a long time ago, Sierra hooked her foot around Paul's ankle and, with a quick jerk, toppled him to the sand.

He was so startled that he sat for a moment, his ego obviously flattened that Sierra had managed to bring him down so quickly. Sierra took off running in the sand, laughing into the night wind. Paul was a much faster runner and overtook her in only a few yards. He grabbed her by the shoulders and pushed her toward the water, playfully threatening to "feed her to the fish." Their laughter echoed off the rocks that formed the end of the bay. The sand ended there, and the only way to reach the sand on the other side of the cliffs was to wade through the rocky tide pools that jutted out between the two beaches. So Paul and Sierra turned around and headed back to the center of the bay, the wind in their faces.

"I love being here with you," Sierra called out over the wind. Then she impulsively put her arm around Paul's waist and welcomed his arm around her waist.

Paul stopped walking and took Sierra in his arms, wrapping her in a tight hug. She felt warmed all over. It lasted only a minute, and then Paul let go. He didn't hold her hand or put his arm around her again but took off at a sprint across the sand.

Sierra laughed and started to run after him. And she had thought she was the impulsive, moody one. It appeared that, in melancholy Paul, she had met her match.

They arrived breathless back at the stairs, grabbed their sandals, and climbed up to the yard, out of the rush of the wind. Sierra brushed back her tangled hair with her free hand and said, "Paul, wait. Stop." She stood alone on the grass. "Look up. Isn't it beautiful?"

Paul didn't return to the grass to join her but looked up from where he stood on the patio. "Spectacular," he said quietly.

"What if we just stayed out here all night and watched the stars together?" Sierra said, smiling at Paul.

Paul gave her a strange look and said, "We need to go in."

"Wait, I wanted to ask you something," Sierra said, joining him on the patio.

"What is it?"

"Well, can we sit down?"

Paul moved the lounge chair back a foot or so from the chair where Sierra landed. He slowly sat down and folded his hands, waiting for Sierra to speak.

She couldn't understand why all the closeness and snuggling was suddenly over. "I just wondered if you've figured out your schedule for the fall."

The last time she and Paul had talked about it, he had

planned to keep working at the construction site where he had been employed all summer, make good money, and take one or two evening classes at the community college. That way he would have enough saved up by the second semester to attend Rancho Corona. Paul's plan was similar to Amy's, only Paul would be less than an hour's drive away from Rancho, and he and Sierra could see each other every weekend.

"I'm registered for sociology on Monday nights," Paul said. "And I'm the first one on the waiting list for a statistics class on Tuesday and Thursday nights. I can take it at another school on Wednesday nights, but it costs twice as much."

"Good. I'm glad your weekends will still be free," Sierra said, leaning back and looking up at the stars.

As she lay in the guest bed now, looking up at the silver flecks in the ceiling, she remembered Paul's answer had made her feel even more distanced from him.

"We'll see" was all he said. Then he stood up and announced, "I'm going in."

Sierra rose and followed him across the patio. For the last several hours she had been imagining what it would be like when they said good night. Sierra thought for sure Paul would kiss her before the night was over. She was certainly ready to kiss him.

But he didn't kiss her. Instead, he briskly led her around to the side door that let them into the house through the garage.

Once inside, he quickly drank a glass of water, as if he were dehydrated. Sierra filled a glass for herself and awkwardly waited around. She thought Paul would at least hug her or somehow say good night in a romantic way. But he didn't. He seemed to be pulling away. As soon as he put the glass in the sink, he turned to Sierra and, with a quick nod, whispered, "Sleep well." Then he turned and left through the dining room while she stood alone in the kitchen.

As Sierra reviewed the details of their time together, she couldn't think of one thing she had said that would have made him pull away. Maybe he realized how late it was, and he was concerned about getting her in trouble with her parents. If she had been at home, her parents would never have agreed to let her stay out that late.

Sierra knew that was about to change. She was going to be the one to set her own curfew now, and if she and Paul wanted to stay out and walk on the beach until the sun came up, that would be their decision. The thought was very satisfying.

She strained to read the luminous green numbers of the alarm clock on the dresser—2:27. Tomorrow would be another full day. She had to try to sleep. The worship service at Paul's church would come early in the morning, and after that was the reception for Tawni and Jeremy in the church fellowship hall. During it all, Paul and Sierra would be together.

As it turned out, Paul and Sierra were indeed "together" all day Sunday, but no one observing the two would have guessed they were acquainted, let alone friends who were close enough to walk along the beach holding hands. Paul managed to keep his distance from her all day. They sat next to each other during the church service, but Paul literally put the hymnbook between them. Sierra went from being mystified to being angry. By the time the grand reception was over and the two families were ready to wearily go their separate ways for the evening, Sierra had a long string of angry words all lined up for Paul.

"You ready to go?" her dad asked, tagging Sierra's arm in the church parking lot. "The boys are on their way to the van."

Sierra was waiting to see what Paul was going to do. He was still inside the church, probably taking down the last of the tables in the fellowship hall. All during the reception Paul had been running around, fixing things, unlocking cupboards with his dad's keys, and answering questions for the women who handled the refreshments. He barely had stopped the whole time and hadn't spoken to Sierra at all.

Then a thought washed over her. Maybe she wasn't being fair. Paul was more or less "on duty," since he was trying to make things go smoothly for his brother, and he was the pastor's son who knew where everything was.

"Sierra," her dad said when she didn't move, "are you coming with us?"

Softened by her revelation, Sierra wanted to talk to Paul. Even if she couldn't talk to him, maybe she could help put away tables so she could at least be with him. "I think I'll go with Paul, Dad," Sierra announced. "You guys go ahead."

"Are you sure Paul is planning to drive all the way up to his grandparents' tonight? I thought he had to be at work early tomorrow, so he was going to stay at his parents' house."

Sierra hadn't counted on that. "I'd better go ask him," she said. "Do you mind?" She turned and met her dad's gaze.

She must have given him a look of overeagerness about

to turn into panic because he spoke to her softly. "Honey, if Paul was planning to take you back to his grandparents' house, I think he would have mentioned it by now."

Sierra felt like bursting into tears but refused to do so. "It will only take me two minutes to go ask him," she said.

Her dad nodded sympathetically. "Two minutes."

Sierra charged back into the church gym and immediately spotted Paul with a long broom in his hand, sweeping the floor. He looked up when she came in and gave her enough of a smile that she felt she could march across the floor and speak her mind.

The incident reminded her of when she worked at the Highland House her junior year. It was a halfway house that Paul's uncle ran in Portland. Sierra had helped out at the Highland House when Paul worked there as well. They didn't have much of a relationship then, and they didn't speak to each other much, but Sierra remembered feeling as if Paul were watching her. It had intimidated her.

Today she refused to be intimidated—especially by a guy who had written his heart to her for months and had only 24 hours earlier held her so tenderly on the beach and quoted poetry he had written for her alone.

Whatever the reason was for Paul's aloofness, Sierra was going to find out. She wasn't going to Rancho Corona tomorrow morning without things being settled between them.

chapter eleven

"**A**RE YOU GOING BACK TO YOUR GRANDPARENTS' house?" Sierra asked while still a few feet away from Paul.

"No, I hadn't planned on it."

"Oh," Sierra said, not sure if she should be mad or understanding, since he did have to start work early tomorrow.

Paul leaned on the broom handle, and Sierra took a deep breath. Before she could let her words come out, Paul said, "Sierra, we need to talk."

"Funny," she said, "that's exactly what I was going to tell you."

"I want to be honest with you," Paul said, glancing around as if to make sure no one could hear him. "I'm not exactly ready to have this talk with you because I haven't decided what I want to say yet."

"Well, when do you think you'll be ready? Because as it stands, my dad's waiting for me, and tomorrow morning I go to Rancho. You work all week, so what does that give us? Next weekend maybe? Do you think you can figure out what you want to say to me by next weekend?"

Paul looked surprised by Sierra's words. Or maybe it

wasn't the words but the angry, sarcastic tone she used to say them.

"I'm sorry," Sierra said. "It's just that I'm so upset with you right now I don't know what to say. Last night I thought everything was wonderful and close, and I was completely open with you, Paul. And you were close and wonderful and open with me, too." Sierra fought hard to keep back the tears. "Suddenly, you act as if I have the plague. You won't talk to me, you won't touch me or look me in the eye—"

"I'm looking you in the eye now," Paul said with his clear, blue-gray eyes fixed on her.

Sierra looked into his eyes and didn't look away. With her voice much softer and lower, she said, "What is the problem, Paul? What happened?"

Paul pressed his lips together, still looking into Sierra's eyes. "We got going too fast. I was afraid."

"Afraid of what?"

"Afraid of things between us getting out of control."

Sierra didn't understand. They had held hands and sat close and snuggled. He had recited his poem to her. They had laughed and gazed at stars together. How was any of that "out of control"?

"I've been there before, Sierra. Please trust me when I say I didn't want that to happen to us."

"You didn't want *what* to happen to us?"

"You know," Paul said, scanning her face, as if looking for assurance that she understood the deeper meaning of his words. "Physically," Paul finally said. "I didn't want things to get out of control between us physically."

Sierra was still in the dark. "How could they have gotten out of control?" She lowered her voice to almost a whisper. "You didn't even kiss me."

"I know," Paul said, looking relieved. "And you'll never know how glad I am that I didn't."

If Paul had slapped her across the jaw, it would have hurt less than his words and the deeper meaning she read in his facial expression. Flinching, Sierra pulled back. "I see." She looked away.

"Do you really?" Paul tilted his head and gave Sierra a charming, innocent look.

Just then Mr. Jensen called from across the empty gym floor, "Sierra, we need to get going. I have the boys waiting in the van. We need to go now."

Sierra wouldn't allow herself the luxury of one more view of Paul's blue-gray eyes or his broad forehead and wavy, brown hair, even though her heart was telling her it would be her last look. She kept her eyes down as she turned away from him. "Good-bye, Paul," she managed to say as she hurried to join her father at the other side of the gym.

"Call me!" Paul hollered as she left the gym. "Call me when you get your new number at Rancho."

"Everything okay?" Mr. Jensen asked, slipping his arm around Sierra as they walked quickly to the waiting family members in the hot van.

"Sure," Sierra said flatly. Inwardly, she was building a mighty dam of determination to hold back all her feelings for the rest of her life. She had been naive to give her heart so quickly to Paul. He flat out didn't want her. He didn't like her the way she liked him. She had made a fool of herself, and he had played along with it, writing poems that he knew she would like to hear, holding her hand because he knew she wanted him to. It had all been a big lie. All his words in all those letters. All the dreams she had stored up. It was all a big nothing. A long, elaborate joke played out on inexperienced Sierra. And the punch line was, "You'll never know how glad I am I didn't kiss you."

There. Now it was over. Ha-ha. So this was why people wrote songs about love and cheating hearts and broken dreams. It was all real now—too painfully real. All Sierra could think of was the time Amy said to her, "I promise I'll be there for you when Paul breaks your heart."

Sierra, of course, had assured Amy that would never happen because Sierra knew what she was doing. Now here she was, finding enough hidden strength from somewhere deep inside that she could walk silently beside her father across the church parking lot and act as if a sinkhole of despair hadn't just opened up and swallowed her whole.

Somehow Sierra managed to keep up the act the rest of that night and into the next day when her father drove her to Rancho. Twice Wesley asked her if something was bothering her, but Sierra said she was nervous about moving into the dorms and going away to college and everything. She didn't know if he believed her or not.

Mr. Jensen moved Sierra's belongings into her room, but before they had finished he said, "Don't forget to call Paul. He said he wanted you to call as soon as you got your new number."

Sierra only vaguely remembered Paul's calling out those words at the church gym. The person she wanted to call was Vicki. Sierra wanted to try to persuade Vicki to come down as soon as she could. Classes didn't start for more than a week, and Sierra didn't want to be alone in their dorm room. Without a car or a roommate, Sierra suddenly realized she was facing a lonely week. In her original plans, this time was going to be filled with Paul during every one of his spare moments.

Walking her dad down to the men's dorm, where Wes was unloading Randy's band equipment, Sierra thanked her father for all he had done to get her to college and to set up her room. To her surprise, he slipped his strong hand over Sierra's and held it as they walked. "You're going to be just fine, Sierra Mae. Your mother and I are the ones who are going to have trouble making the adjustments. It's probably a good thing she flew back with Granna Mae this morning. If she had come here and tried to say good-bye to both you and Wesley on the heels of Tawni's engagement, well, I think it would have been hard to convince her we should stay in Portland. She would have wanted to move down here—especially after she saw this campus. It's exactly as Wes and you described it."

They were walking past the plaza fountain at the center of the campus, still holding hands. Sierra didn't mind that several other early-bird students who sat at the benches surrounding the fountain were watching. She guessed that any one of the three girls sitting there would love to have a dad like Sierra's.

Suddenly, one of the girls on the bench called her name. Sierra stopped, and both she and her dad turned. The long-legged girl who rose from the bench and eagerly came toward them had a bright, welcoming smile. Her long, nutmeg brown hair was pulled back in a braid, and she wore sunglasses, which kept Sierra from recognizing her. The girl wore shorts and a short-sleeved T-shirt, and when she raised her arm to wave at Sierra, the sun glistened off a gold ID bracelet on her right wrist.

"Christy!" Screaming, Sierra ran to hug her dear friend. "I can't believe you're here! How are you? When did you get back from Switzerland?"

Christy hugged Sierra a second time and took off her sunglasses, revealing her distinctive blue-green eyes. They sparkled when they saw Sierra. "It's so good to see you," Christy said, taking a closer look at Sierra's left eye.

"I had a run-in with a can of root beer," Sierra explained. "It's actually lots better than it was a couple of days ago."

Christy smiled. "Katie is going to want to hear the whole story. Did she ever tell you about the time on the houseboat when Doug gave her a black eye?"

"No, but I'm sure with very little prompting she'll tell me the whole story. Oh, Christy, this is my dad."

"I'm pleased to meet you, Mr. Jensen," Christy said, offering her hand to him.

"It's a pleasure meeting you," Mr. Jensen said, shaking Christy's hand. Sierra felt so grown up. Her friends in high school never shook hands with her parents. Christy seemed even more grown up. Sierra hadn't seen her friend for more than a year, ever since the two of them had gone to Switzerland with Christy's aunt so Christy could check out the school she ended up going to for the past year.

"Is Todd here?" Sierra asked.

"You just missed him. He and my parents picked me up at the airport a few days ago, and then he stayed with us and helped me move in earlier today. He'll be back." Christy smiled when she said it. "He's going to work the rest of this week and then move into the dorm on Friday."

Sierra felt a bittersweetness come over her. If things weren't going to work out between Paul and her, at least she could be happy for Christy that she and Todd were together. Sierra would have to ask Christy exactly how many years she and Todd had been together. Five? Or was it six? Either one was amazing, especially since Sierra couldn't manage to maintain a dating relationship for even five to six hours.

"Katie should be here this afternoon," Christy added.

"You know," Mr. Jensen said, "I can find my way from here, Sierra."

"You sure?" Sierra asked.

"Yes, I'm sure. Let me give you a hug, and I'll be on my way."

Sierra hugged him tightly and whispered in his ear, "Good-bye, Daddy. I love you. Thanks again for everything."

"I love you, too," he whispered back.

As Sierra pulled away, she could see that her dad was "overly" smiling, and the lines by his eyes were crinkling the way they did when he was trying not to cry.

"You okay?" Sierra asked quietly.

He nodded and kissed her soundly on the cheek. Then he turned and headed for the men's dorms.

"I just said good-bye to my dad," Sierra said solemnly as she turned her attention back to Christy. "I didn't think it would be like that."

"Do you want to go with him?" Christy asked.

"No."

"You sure?"

Sierra watched her dad's familiar gait another minute

as he turned down a path behind the library. Then he was gone.

"So many good-byes," Sierra said as a sense of loss came over her.

Christy gave Sierra's arm a squeeze. "And many hellos, too."

Sierra smiled at her understanding friend. "If all the good-byes don't kill me, I'll probably start to enjoy some of these hellos."

"I know what you mean," Christy said. "Come on. I brought you something from Switzerland. It's in my room, and it just might cheer you up."

"You brought me something?"

"Yep. And I know you're going to like it." Christy flipped her sunglasses back on and led Sierra toward the upperclassmen dorm. Sierra couldn't imagine what Christy had brought her, but she did know she was going to like being around Christy and Katie and all their friends. For the first time, the thought crossed her mind that maybe Paul truly was a "good-bye," and some guy at Rancho Corona was going to be her newest "hello."

chapter twelve

CHRISTY'S DORM ROOM WAS COMPLETELY SET UP ON the left side. The right side had only an unmade bed, an empty closet, an empty desk, and vacant bookshelves. Christy was already at home here, and Katie would have to catch up when she arrived.

"Wow, you settled in fast," Sierra said, examining some of the pictures on the wall. Next to the window was a framed poster of a tropical waterfall with a quaint bridge across the top of it. At the bottom of the frame was what looked like a piece of fabric that had been cut from a T-shirt. It read, *I Survived the Hana Road.*

Next to the desk was another framed poster. This was a more familiar scene to Sierra: a mountain trail in the Alps, complete with cows wearing bells around their necks, snow-capped peaks, and a colorful carpet of blue, yellow, and white wildflowers.

"This looks like where we had our picnic with Alex," Sierra said.

"I know," Christy responded. "That's why I bought it. I went back to that same spot several times this past year. And each time I thought about you and Alex and his verses about loving each other fervently."

Sierra smiled at the memory. *See?* she told herself. *Other guys in the world have been interested in you. Paul isn't the only one.*

"Did I tell you I saw Alex last month? He was visiting his uncle at the school, and guess what? He's engaged!"

Cross Alex off my list of potential interests, Sierra thought dismally. "That's great," she said generously. "He deserves someone wonderful. Did I tell you my sister and Jeremy just got engaged? We had a big family party this weekend."

"I take it you finally saw Paul," Christy said, reaching for a tiny white box on the shelf above her desk. Sierra noticed it was next to a beat-up metal Folgers coffee can, which Christy had placed on a white lace doily. Sierra made a mental note to ask Christy why in the world she had a funky old can in a place of honor.

"Yes, I finally saw Paul. And it was both wonderful and horrible, and if I start to talk about it, I'll cry."

"Well, here," Christy said, holding out the tiny white box. "See if this brings back any sweet memories. It got a little squished in my suitcase. Sorry."

Sierra opened the tiny box and found three exquisitely decorated pieces of chocolate candy. "Truffles! From that bakery we went to with your aunt, right? I can't believe you remembered."

"I was going to try to bring home one of their pastries, but the truffles fit in my suitcase better. Remember when we sat on that bench in the sunshine and had our first bites of amazing Swiss chocolate?"

"Oh, do I! And your aunt told us we couldn't chew them but had to savor the moment and let the chocolate dissolve in our mouths." Sierra broke off a corner of one of the squished truffles and offered the box to Christy so she could take a piece. Before popping it into her mouth, Sierra added, "And remember how mad your aunt was because we knocked over the card rack at that shop across the street? I still have one of the mangled cards she had to buy. I think I brought it with me. I should put it up on my wall."

Christy laughed and pointed to the large bulletin board next to her closet. "Look; there's mine." Sure enough, in the top right corner was a card with a crease right down the middle of an illustration of a wildflower bouquet.

Sierra laughed and held her piece of chocolate up in the air. Christy did the same. "On the count of three," Sierra said. "One, two, three!"

The two friends lowered the precious chocolate into their mouths and slowly let it melt, echoing a duet of "mmm's" and "ahhh's."

Christy plopped onto her bed and moved a stuffed Winnie the Pooh from on top of her pillow. "I'm sure going to miss that bakery," she said.

Sierra made herself comfy on the foot of Christy's bed. She noticed how soft the comforter was. It was a faded yellow patchwork design, and Sierra guessed it probably held sentimental appeal for Christy because it didn't match anything else in the room. Looking up at the dresser, Sierra noticed a vase filled with white carnations. She assumed they were a welcome-home bouquet from Todd.

"What else are you going to miss about Switzerland?" Sierra asked.

Christy gazed out the window before answering. "I'm not sure I even know yet. It was my life for a year, and now all of a sudden I'm here. I don't think it's all hit me."

"Didn't you miss Todd fiercely?"

"Yes and no. I needed to grow up some and settle some things in my heart before I could move on in my relationship with Todd. And he needed to do some growing up, too. He kept changing schools and majors. He had a bunch of jobs but never anything consistent—and he never had any money. He needed time to make some decisions, too."

"Katie told me awhile ago that Todd's been working like a crazy man. She thought he was trying to save enough so you guys could get married."

Christy's calm, gentle face took on a determined look. "Todd needs to graduate first. That's his goal in coming to Rancho this year. He's decided he wants to be a youth pastor."

"I can see him doing that. He's a great teacher, and a natural leader. I would have loved for him to be my youth pastor when I was in junior high," Sierra said. "Sounds like a good choice."

Christy nodded. "It does. He'll be a great youth pastor. It just took him awhile to come to that conclusion. For so many years he wanted to be a missionary in some tropical jungle, live in a tree house, and eat coconuts."

Sierra laughed. "You're kidding."

"No. That's exactly what he wanted to do. You can ask him."

"What changed his mind?"

"God."

"Oh," Sierra said.

"And it wasn't an easy task, from my point of view." Christy adjusted her pillow behind her and smiled. "Todd wanted to be a Bible translator, but he doesn't have a natural ear for languages. He tried taking some linguistics classes but had to drop them because he just couldn't get it. Then he signed up with a missions organization, thinking they would send him to Papua New Guinea, and they sent him to Spain instead."

"That's where you saw him when you and I first met on the missions trip at Carnforth Hall."

"Exactly," Christy said. "It's been a long journey for Todd to figure out what God wants him to do, and I think it was easier for Todd to go through that process while I was far away."

"Now what?" Sierra asked.

Christy shrugged. She didn't look distressed, just hopeful and dreamy. "We just 'keep on keeping on,' as the director of the orphanage in Basel used to say. It was so wonderful being together these last few days when Todd was at my parents' house and helped me move in here. Now we're going to see each other every day. I don't want to start making any predictions, though. We need to take each day as it comes."

Sierra reached for the white candy box on the desk, and after taking another truffle, she offered the last bite to Christy. Since Christy had been so open about her relationship with Todd, Sierra felt compelled to tell Christy about her wonderful-horrible weekend with Paul.

As soon as the piece of chocolate melted, Sierra drew in a deep breath and said, "I'm really glad everything is working out between Todd and you. I guess I should tell you that all my dreams about Paul crashed and burned yesterday."

"Do you want to tell me about it?" Christy asked. "I mean, I'd really like to hear, but only if you want to tell me."

Christy was two years older than Sierra, which made

her the same age as Tawni. But Sierra had never thought
of Christy in the same way she thought of her sister. Christy
was more of an equal, a close friend, yet more experienced
and therefore a wise counselor.

"He basically acted as though I was his girlfriend on
Saturday and then ignored me on Sunday and said he
didn't want to ever see me again."

Christy looked surprised. "He told you that?"

"Well . . ." Sierra tried to make her emotions pull back
so she could relay the information accurately. "Not exactly.
That's what it felt like. You see, on Saturday night we
walked on the beach, and he held me and quoted a poem
he had written just for me. I'm telling you, Christy, I was
sure this was 'it,' you know? This had to be what it felt like
to be in love, and nothing could ever break us up. I was
so . . . so . . ."

"Vulnerable?" Christy filled in for her.

"Okay. Yes, vulnerable. And happy. I was so sure of my
feelings."

"And you gave him your heart," Christy suggested.

Sierra nodded.

"And he took your heart in his hand, and with a
friendly smile but a critical eye, he scanned it, then set it
down and said, 'It is still unripe, better wait awhile.' "

"Where did you get those words?"

"From a Christina Rossetti poem. I have it copied in
my diary. I went through the same thing with Todd a long
time ago. But I still remember how much it hurt. I'm sorry
you're going through this, Sierra. It doesn't necessarily
mean everything is over between the two of you, though."

"I don't know," Sierra said, kicking off her sandals and
sitting on the bed with her legs tucked under her. "Paul

said I would never know how glad he was that he didn't kiss me. That feels pretty terminal to me."

"Why did he say that?"

"He said things were going too fast, and he didn't want things between us to get out of control physically because he had been there before."

"Did he mean he had been in a physical relationship?"

"I guess. But how could things be going too fast and becoming too involved for us? All we did was hold hands. He didn't even kiss me!" Sierra was picking up steam as she released her emotions. "How can hugging and holding hands be too involved? I think he was saying all that as an excuse to cover up what he really meant. He doesn't care for me the way I care for him. He doesn't want to be around me."

"Sierra, holding hands and hugging are the first steps, you know. It can be hard to pull back once you're familiar with each other that way. Paul obviously knows where his guidelines and standards are in a relationship. Are you sure that's not what he was trying to communicate? That he had a line he didn't want to cross physically in your relationship?"

Sierra refused to accept such a simple explanation. "But why would he say he was so glad he didn't kiss me?"

"Obviously, kissing is the next step, and he wasn't ready to go there."

"I was," Sierra said. "It was such a romantic evening. It would have been the perfect place and time for my first kiss."

"But, Sierra, think about it. You guys went from nothing to step one, holding hands, and on to step two, hugging, in just a few hours. It sounds to me as if Paul wanted to pull back and take things more slowly. I think that was really kind of him."

In Sierra's mind, she saw Paul sitting like a rock on the second step of a long, winding staircase. His arms were folded across his chest as if to say stubbornly, "This is as far as I'm going, Sierra. Take it or leave it." Her heart began to melt. Why hadn't she seen that before? If he didn't care for her so much, he wouldn't have stopped on the second step. How could she have misinterpreted everything so badly?

"You know what, Christy? You're right. I had it all backward." Sierra remembered how Paul had looked, standing in the church gym, leaning on the broom, his head tilted with that charmingly shy expression on his face. He had looked so innocent. Just like the toddler with the gray eyes that Jalene had held on her hip at Mama Bear's.

"I admire Paul for treating you that way," Christy said. "Especially since he's apparently been further up the steps in other relationships."

Suddenly, the image of Paul planted like a rock on the second step disappeared, and a new, disturbing image took its place. Paul was on an escalator, running up the steps. Another girl was running up the steps with him. That other girl was Jalene.

chapter thirteen

"OH, CHRISTY, I THINK I'M GOING TO BE SICK."
Sierra slid off the bed and curled herself up in a ball on the floor, hugging her legs to her chest.

"What is it? What's wrong? Was it the chocolate?"

"No, no, no!" Sierra moaned.

Christy sat on the floor beside her and gently touched her arm. "Sierra, what is it?"

Sierra lifted her head and faced Christy, trying to make the escalator image in her imagination go away. "I should have seen this before. Why didn't I guess? I am so naive!"

Christy reached for a tissue and handed it to Sierra even though she didn't have any visible tears.

"No wonder Paul said he wasn't ready to talk. He said he didn't know what he wanted to say to me. He knew I didn't know, and that's why he said he didn't want things to get out of control. He said he had been there before. He asked me to trust him when he said he didn't want that to happen to us."

"Paul didn't want *what* to happen?"

Sierra looked away from her concerned friend and spoke the words she didn't want to hear herself say. "Paul's last girlfriend got pregnant. They obviously went to the top of the stairs. I've seen her baby—Paul's baby. He has gray eyes and tilts his head just like . . ." Sierra couldn't finish. The tears she had been holding back came gushing out. She buried her face in her raised knees and let the tears flow.

"Oh, Christy," Sierra said at last, "how could I have been so blind?" She sniffed and choked out the words. "Paul wasn't walking with the Lord when he dated Jalene. No wonder he left for a year and ran away to Scotland. When he was planning to come to Portland for my graduation, he said he had a few people he needed to set things right with. He must have meant Jalene and their son. He wanted to see their son!"

Another wave of frantic tears washed over Sierra, and she exhausted herself with the emotional outburst. The worst part was that the excessive crying made her left eye ache around the bruise, and she was sure it was beginning to swell again.

Christy sat quietly beside Sierra and let her cry. Several times Christy handed Sierra tissues, and twice she stroked Sierra's wild, curly mane in a gesture of understanding.

When the last of Sierra's tears had been released, she looked up and tried to breathe deeply. She had just regained control of her emotions when they heard a key being inserted into the door's lock. A second later the door flew open, and boisterous, red-haired Katie burst inside.

"Home sweet . . . Sierra? What's wrong?" Katie dropped the box in her arms and flew to Sierra's side. "What happened to your eye? Are you okay? Christy, what's going on?"

Christy quietly stood and pulled Katie along with her.

"Come on. I'll help you unload your stuff and carry it in."
Then, turning to Sierra, Christy asked, "Do you want me
to tell Katie or would you rather tell her later?"

Sierra pointed at Christy. "You tell her. I don't think I
can."

Katie and Christy left, closing the door behind them.

"Oh, Father God," Sierra mumbled in the still room,
"I never expected anything like this. Why didn't You warn
me? Why didn't You make me pull back a long time ago?
I put so much hope and trust in Paul. I never expected . . ."

The phone on the desk rang. Sierra jumped. It rang
again, and she thought she should answer it. Clearing her
throat and reaching for the receiver, Sierra said, "Hello?"

"Hi, I'm not sure I have the right room," the male voice
said on the other end. "Is this Katie?"

"No, but she'll be right back." The voice sounded so
familiar that Sierra had to venture a guess. "Is this Wes?"

"Sierra?"

"Yeah. What are you doing calling Katie?"

"I was trying to find you, since you didn't answer the
phone in your room. I remembered you knew Katie from
when we visited in the spring, and I guessed you might be
there."

"Well, I am here," Sierra said, reaching for another
tissue. She tried to blow her nose quietly.

"Dad left a little while ago," Wes said. "I wondered if
you wanted to meet me at the student coffee shop for some
lunch."

"I'm not very hungry," Sierra said.

Wes paused and then said, "Are you okay?"

Sierra wasn't sure if she should be open with her
brother or not. She decided she should say something but

not too much. "I just figured some things out, and they hit me kind of hard."

"You mean about being on your own now?"

"No."

"Is it anything you want to talk about?"

Sierra sighed deeply. "I've been talking to Christy. She's Katie's roommate. She's the one I went to Switzerland with."

"Well, I won't interrupt then. But if you feel like calling, I'm at extension 3232."

"That's an easy number to remember."

"Call me later if you want. I'm going to get something to eat."

Sierra hung up and looked around the room. She felt dizzy. Or maybe she *was* hungry, and lunch with Wes would have done her some good. Before she could reconsider meeting him at the coffee shop, Christy and Katie reappeared, both carrying large boxes, which they promptly lowered to the floor.

"You guys need some help?" Sierra said, scooping up her crumpled tissues and looking for a wastebasket.

"If you want my opinion," Katie said, her green eyes flashing above her rosy cheeks, "I say, 'Big whoop.'"

"Big whoop?"

"I told her everything," Christy said.

"Yeah, big whoop. Whatever happened with Paul and his old girlfriend is in the past. He wasn't a Christian then, was he? Or, if he was, he was totally backsliding from what I remember your saying about him. So whatever happened in the past is the past. God forgave all that stuff when Paul came back to Him. If God isn't holding it against Paul, then none of us should hold it against him, either."

"You haven't even met Paul," Sierra said.

"But he's a brother in Christ, right? So the Bible says I'm to forgive others as Christ has forgiven me. You can't hold this against him, Sierra. That would be so unfair."

"But Katie, a few other lives are involved in this."

"Remember what Jesus said when He was hanging on the cross for us? He said, 'Father, forgive them. They don't know what they're doing.' Every day people make mistakes. They don't have any idea what they're doing. If they ask God to forgive them, then we're supposed to forgive them as well. Don't you remember that verse on the wall at Carnforth Hall: 'Love will cover a multitude of sins.'"

"Actually, it says, 'Love bears all things, believes all things, hopes all things, and endures all things. Love never fails,'" Christy said.

"Well, both of those love quotes are from the Bible," Katie said, wiping the perspiration that had beaded up on her forehead. "My point is, Sierra, what does it matter? Does Paul's past have anything to do with your future?"

"I don't know." Sierra felt as if all the wind had been knocked out of her. "I don't know much of anything at this moment."

"Maybe we should all eat something," Christy suggested. "It's after 2:00, and I don't know about you, but breakfast was a long time ago for me."

"Let's finish unloading my car," Katie said. "Then we can all drive into town for some food. I want to stop at a drugstore, too. I don't have any shampoo."

The three of them worked quickly, hauling several heavy boxes out of the heat into the air-conditioned comfort of the room. Sierra had never seen Katie's car before, and she thought the bright yellow vehicle was perfect for

Katie. It was a cross between a Jeep and a dune buggy. Katie called it "Baby Hummer."

Sierra, Christy, and Katie all climbed into Baby Hummer after they had stacked the boxes on Katie's side of the room and drove down the hill into the town of Temecula. They all agreed on the first fast-food place they came to and ate in the car on the way to the drugstore. Sierra bought some toothpaste, a box of snack bars, and a bottle of apple juice. After Katie collected a small basketful of necessities, she and Sierra went searching for Christy.

They found her in the laundry soap aisle looking dazed. "Look at all these boxes of soap," Christy muttered. "How do you know what to buy? In Switzerland I had only three brands to choose from. There are so many choices here. Liquid or powder? Do I need fabric softener? What is this color-safe bleach? And do I need a stain remover?"

"She's losing it," Katie confided to Sierra. "I knew it would catch up with her real soon. She's been back only a few days, you know."

"Jet lag?" Sierra questioned.

Katie shook her head and took Christy by the arm, leading her to the checkout stand. "Cultural reentry," she said. "It's really bad on missionaries who have been in remote areas for a long time. They forget what a land of abundance America is."

"There are just so many choices," Christy said again.

"We learned about this last semester in my intercultural studies class," Katie informed Sierra. Turning to Christy, she said, "You'll freak out if you stay in this store much longer, Christy. Let's go back to the dorm and unpack my stuff. We can buy you some laundry soap tomorrow."

Back at the dorm, Christy seemed to have lost all her

energy. She blamed that on the jet lag and afternoon heat.

"You guys, I'm going to bed," Christy said, crawling under her covers with her clothes still on.

"Will it bother you if I unpack?" Katie asked.

Christy didn't answer. She appeared to already be asleep.

"I'll stay and help if you want me to," Sierra said in a low voice.

"That would be great. Are you already moved in?"

"Not really. My side of the room looks just like this, all boxes. Vicki doesn't arrive until the end of the week. To be honest, I'd rather stay here than go back to my room right now."

"Then stay all night," Katie suggested. "In one of these boxes, I have an air mattress. If you don't mind sleeping on the floor, it's all yours."

They set to work, talking about school, parents, their summer jobs, and their expectations for the coming school year. Several times they started to laugh and then remembered Christy was trying to sleep, so they lowered their voices and tried to be quiet. It didn't seem to matter, though. Christy was in a deep sleep.

Sierra appreciated that Katie didn't bring up anything about Paul. It gave Sierra a chance to even out her emotions.

Since Katie didn't have a lot of treasures to hang on the wall, it didn't take long to set up her side of the room. Sierra was beginning to understand why Wes had said a few boxes of belongings turned into valuable treasures when that's all a person had of home and the past. It made Sierra eager to unpack her boxes—but not tonight. Tonight she would cheer herself with the warmth of Katie's energetic personality. Sierra would have tomorrow to make her own little nest cozy.

She slept well on the air mattress and borrowed a clean T-shirt from Katie the next morning before the three of them went to the coffee shop in search of breakfast.

"When does the cafeteria start to serve meals?" Sierra asked.

"Thursday dinner is the first meal," Katie said.

"I'm going to go broke before then," Sierra said as she paid for her bagel and orange juice.

"I know," Christy said with a yawn. "I just can't seem to wake up, you guys."

"There's no reason you can't go back to bed," Katie said. "Nothing is going on today."

"I thought we were going to help Sierra set up her room."

"There's not that much to do," Sierra said. "You should sleep while you can. This seems like the quiet before the storm."

Just as Sierra said it, her brother entered the side door of the coffee shop. He noticed her right away and marched over to their table. He didn't look happy.

chapter fourteen

"WHERE HAVE YOU BEEN, SIERRA?" WES looked more angry than worried.

"I've been with these guys. Katie, you know my brother Wes. Wes, this is Christy."

Christy held out her hand to shake with Wes. He shook quickly and then looked back at Sierra. "Didn't you go back to your room last night?"

"No. I stayed on the floor in Katie and Christy's room."

Wes looked flustered. "Then will you do me a favor and give Mom a call and then call Paul?" He handed Sierra a slip of paper with a phone number on it. "He's called me four times since I got here yesterday, trying to track you down. You were supposed to call him and give him your number."

"I, um . . ." Sierra stalled, feeling embarrassed that her brother was chewing her out in front of her friends. She felt as if she were back in junior high and not at all like an independent college woman. "I'm not sure I'm ready to talk to Paul," she said. "Can you tell him that for me, if he calls you again?"

Now Wes was the one who looked embarrassed, as if she had reduced him to a junior high messenger between two friends who weren't speaking to each other. "And why can't you tell him that?"

"I . . ." Sierra couldn't answer.

Just then some of Katie's friends walked up and visited with her for a few minutes. It gave Wes a chance to cool down. He pulled up a chair and sat on it backward, leaning his arms on the backrest at the end of the table next to Sierra. Then he reached over and took half of Sierra's bagel and chomped into it.

"Hey, I paid for that!" Sierra said. "And I'm on a very tight budget. Go buy your own bagel."

"Okay, okay. I'll buy you a bagel." Wes took another bite and rose to order some food. "Anyone else want anything?"

"See if they have any of those little packets of peanut butter," Katie said. "Smooth, not crunchy."

As soon as Katie's friends left, and while Wes was still waiting for his bagel, Katie leaned toward Sierra and said, "Are you going to tell Wes about Paul?"

"I don't know. It's starting to bug me that Wes is checking up on me."

"I think you should tell him," Katie said. "Otherwise he's going to be caught in the middle with Paul calling him and you saying you don't want to talk to him. It's not really fair to Wes, if you're asking him to relay those messages for you."

"Do you agree?" Sierra asked Christy. For a blink of a moment, Sierra felt as if she were back at Mama Bear's with her head bent close around the table with her two friends. Only these two friends weren't college freshmen, like Sierra, Amy, and Vicki. Katie and Christy were both going to be juniors. They had much more experience to draw on when it came to complications with guys.

Christy said, "You know I've been thinking. I know we should speak the truth in love, and the truth would help Wes in this situation. But we shouldn't spread rumors about other people."

"You think I'm making that up about Paul?" Sierra felt her defenses rise. "Is that what it seems like to you? That I'm gossiping and making up a rumor about Paul and Jalene having a baby?"

Christy and Katie both looked over the top of Sierra's head as if signaling her that Wes was returning. She instantly went silent and waited to see if he had overheard her. She suspected her voice had grown a little loud at the end.

Wes sat down. He flipped half of his bagel onto Sierra's paper plate and tossed the peanut butter to Katie. Turning to look at Sierra, he raised his eyebrows as if inviting her to explain what he had just heard.

"Okay," Sierra said with a huff. "I saw Paul's old girl-friend at Mama Bear's the day before we came down here. She had a little toddler with her. After some of the things Paul said this weekend, I just figured out the little boy was his—his and Jalene's. Paul doesn't know that I know yet, and I'm not sure I'm ready to talk to him about everything. He said on Sunday that he wasn't ready to have that conversation with me, and I'm not ready to have it with him, either. Not yet."

Wesley looked skeptical. "Are you sure?"

"Yes, I'm sure. That's why I asked if you could tell him I wasn't ready."

"No, I mean, are you sure Paul and Jalene had a baby? That's pretty intense, Sierra."

"Tell me about it."

"But he wasn't walking with the Lord then," Katie said, slipping into the conversation. "I think if God's forgiven him, then Sierra should forgive him, and they should just go on from there. We should never torture our brothers and sisters in Christ by holding past failures before them."

"You're right," Wes said. Then, turning to Sierra, he added, "And you know what? This is going to get way out of hand unless you have a private conversation with Paul. The sooner the better."

Sierra didn't agree with Wes. He didn't understand how high her hopes had been for her relationship with Paul. Wes would only give her a lecture about why he thought girls should stay "emotional virgins" if she tried to tell him how deeply this revelation about Paul hurt her.

"I think I'd better go," Sierra said, feeling that she would be better off dismissing herself before she said something she would regret. She collected her carton of orange juice and bagel and slid out of the booth.

"I'll walk back to the dorms with you," Christy said.

"Well, I'm staying," Katie said. "I told the guys who were just here that I'd eat with them when they came back. They went to get some money."

Wes gave Sierra a fatherly look, which irritated her. As she and Christy were leaving, he said, "I'll trust you to talk to Paul soon."

"Why did he have to say that?" Sierra muttered as they exited. "And why did I ever think going to the same university as my brother was a good idea?"

Christy didn't answer. They walked across campus in the brightness of the late morning sunshine, and Christy asked Sierra if she wanted to stop at the fountain. At first she didn't want to, but then Christy coaxed her to stop for just a minute. No one else was around, and in the warmth of the day, the coolness of the water was appealing.

Christy slipped off her sandals and stepped into the fountain. Sierra took the last swig of her orange juice and then followed Christy's example. When her feet first touched the smooth blue tiles, the cool water felt shocking. But then she settled in next to Christy on the edge of the fountain wall, and the two of them silently splashed their feet. The sensation seemed to revive both of them.

"I was thinking," Christy said, "did Paul actually say the little boy you saw was his son?"

"No. He doesn't know I saw him."

"Did Paul ever say anything about Jalene's getting pregnant?"

"No. Not exactly. He just said he had been there before and he didn't want us to end up there."

"Well, Sierra, what if the baby you saw wasn't Paul's? I mean, what if it was some other guy's? Or what if Jalene was never pregnant, but she was baby-sitting the day you saw her? Did you think about that? I mean, what if this is all a misunderstanding?" Christy pulled her long brown hair back and twisted it up on top of her head.

Sierra dismissed Christy's suggestions. "Then why would Paul have pulled back from me the way he did, and why would he have said all the things he did about not wanting to lose control physically?"

Christy let her hair go, and it cascaded down her back, untwisting itself as it fell. "I don't know Paul at all, so I don't have any guesses as to why he did or said anything. But I know from talks Todd and I have had that a lot of times it's different for a guy than it is for a girl. Do you know what I mean?"

Sierra shaded her eyes from the sun and tried to look directly at Christy. The sun was shining off the water, causing an extra-bright glare on their faces.

"Like the other night when Todd and I were at my parents' house. It was about 10:00, and everyone else had gone to bed. Todd and I were talking out on the front porch. We were sitting on the top step under this trellis my dad built. A jasmine vine has grown over the trellis, and in the summer, especially at night, it's the most fragrant canopy you can imagine. Todd had his arms around me, and my back was against the side of his chest. You know, like this." Christy demonstrated by leaning against Sierra and resting her head on Sierra's shoulder.

Sierra laughed. "I've got the picture."

"Well, that's just cozy, right? Balmy night, fragrant jasmine, Todd and me back together again after a very long year. And we're talking about cars. Should he sell ol' Gus."

"No, never!" Sierra said.

"Well, that's what we were discussing," Christy continued. "And I was sitting there thinking how cozy and comfortable it was to hear his voice so close to my ear and to be planning together—even though it was just a little thing like cars. We were together, and I was so happy."

"Sounds perfect," Sierra said.

"Right. Because we're women. But you won't believe what happened. Todd leans over and snuggles his nose into my hair above my ear and kisses me right there." Christy points to a spot on her head above her left ear.

Sierra smiled, drawn into the romance of Christy's story.

"And then Todd says to me, 'I can't do this anymore.' Then we got up and went inside. I went to my room, and he went to David's and slept in the sleeping bag on David's floor."

"Why did he do that? Weren't you mad?" Sierra said. "He ruined the beautiful moment you two were having."

Christy smiled. "No, he preserved a beautiful moment rather than creating a moment of regret."

"I don't get it. You were just snuggling."

"I know," Christy said. "But what's cozy snuggling for me can be something much stronger for Todd. I have to understand and honor that, even though I don't feel the same way. It's taken me a long time to figure out that he and I are wired differently. He's a microwave, and I'm a Crock-Pot."

Sierra laughed.

"Todd always says this is the season for us to save, not spend."

"What does that mean?" Sierra pulled her feet from the cool water and felt them tingle as they dried in the sun. Having her feet washed and cooled had brought a refreshing sensation to her whole body. For some reason she thought of Jesus washing the disciples' feet as an act of love for His closest friends. She wondered if Christy's trying to understand Todd's feelings was also a loving act for her closest friend.

"During these years while we're dating, we're holding back physically from each other," Christy said. "Even when we want to express ourselves, we're saving those expressions instead of spending them. I think of it as putting coins in a piggy bank. The only way that bank can be opened is to break it and let everything come pouring out at once."

Sierra could picture Christy and Todd sitting together under the jasmine trellis with imaginary handfuls of coins. They spent a penny or two each as they cuddled, but then, because they stopped, they were able to save their more valuable coins in their "piggy banks."

Christy pulled her feet from the water, too, and swung around to shake them out in the warm sunshine before slipping them back into her sandals. She stood and said playfully, "I can tell you, Miss Sierra, that by the time my wedding night gets here, whoever I marry is going to get one very full piggy bank, if you know what I mean!"

chapter fifteen

S IERRA BURST OUT LAUGHING AT CHRISTY'S COMMENT. She was refreshingly transparent and honest. It made Sierra glad all over again that they would be together this school year.

"Well, maybe I should go buy myself a piggy bank," Sierra teased. She leaned back and scooped up a handful of water, which she splashed all over Christy.

Christy gave a muffled squeal and laughed with her hands up in defense. "Hey, I don't need a cold shower! I told you I have my hormones under control."

They laughed together and headed off to Sierra's dorm room. Overhead a clump of tall palm trees swayed in the breeze, making a swishing sound that Sierra loved. It wasn't quite the same as the wind in the birch trees outside her bedroom window at the house where she grew up, but it was similar enough to make her feel happy and at home at Rancho Corona.

When they reached the dorm, Sierra and Christy went to work opening Sierra's boxes and settling her into her room.

"Do you think it's dumb to have matching bed-spreads?" Sierra asked as she smoothed the deep green comforter on her bed. "Vicki's mom insisted we buy matching bedspreads. We even have matching throw pillows. I noticed Katie and you don't have anything that matches."

"Katie and I didn't have time to think about that," Christy said. "These comforters will look great together. You were smart to pick a solid color because in these small rooms a print might get old real fast."

"Wait until you see what Vicki is bringing. She has a huge beanbag chair, a stereo and speakers, and a little nightstand. It's going to be so crowded in here."

"It will all fit somehow," Christy said.

They worked together another hour before Christy curled up on Sierra's bed and helped herself to a catnap. Sierra took the opportunity to go down the hall to the pay phone so she could call her mom without waking Christy. She reached the answering machine and left a message that she was doing fine, setting up her room, and enjoying her friends.

After she hung up, she looked at the paper in her hand that listed Paul's home phone number. For the first time she realized she couldn't just decide never to see Paul again. Her sister was marrying his brother. Numerous occasions in the next year would bring them together. Whatever she decided to do with this relationship would affect both families as well. It reminded her of the thought she had had on the way to the Mexican restaurant, that nothing happens to us alone. Her life was connected with those of others, which was why it wasn't a good idea to alienate anyone.

Still not ready to have a heart-to-heart talk with Paul, Sierra used her phone card to call Vicki. Vicki wasn't home either, so Sierra left a quick message and then dialed Amy's number, only to get Amy's voice mail. At least Sierra had tried. She would try again this evening when everyone was home from work. Sierra realized she had just used up precious minutes on her phone card, and she had only been given three cards. After the cards, she would have to pay for all her calls. That was a sobering thought.

Christy was still asleep when Sierra went back to the room, so she collected her towel and a change of clothes and acquainted herself with the shower room located half-way down the hall. The shower was industrial-sized and seemed to magnify every sound she made. Sierra thought it was funny and started to sing, enjoying the wacky echo the shower made. But soon she realized playing in the shower was a way to avoid thinking things through while under the influence of warm, pelting shower drops. Maybe that was okay for right now.

Refreshed and clean all over, she returned to her room just as the phone on her desk rang. Christy stirred, but Sierra reached it before Christy could.

"Hi ya. It's Katie. Is Christy with you?"

"Yes. She's taking a little snooze."

"Well, tell her someone came looking for her. I'll send him over to your dorm."

Christy sat up and asked sleepily, "Who is it?"

"It's Katie," Sierra replied. "There's someone here to see you."

"Who?"

"Hey, Katie," Sierra said into the receiver, "Christy wants to know who you're sending over."

"Ask her if tall, blond, and surfer-dude mean anything to her."

Sierra smiled. "It's Todd. He's on his way over here."

"He is?" Christy sat all the way up and opened her eyes wide. "What's he doing here? I thought he wasn't coming until the end of the week."

"Hey, Katie, Christy wants to know why he's here."

"Why is he here?" Katie repeated. "Oh brother! Tell her if she doesn't want him, she can send him back over here, and he can take *me* out to dinner."

Sierra turned to Christy, "Katie said—"

"I could hear her," Christy said. "Tell her never in a million years, and I mean that in a nice way."

Sierra had been holding the phone out and now put it back to her ear. "Did you get that?"

"Yeah, well, just tell her that next time he comes offering food and she's not around, I won't be so diligent about tracking her down. And I mean that in a nice way, too."

Christy borrowed Sierra's brush and started to untangle her long hair.

Sierra laughed and hung up. She began to relay Katie's line to Christy when the phone rang again. It was the switchboard operator in the dorm lobby.

"Is this Sierra Jensen?" the operator asked.

"Yes."

"You have a visitor, Sierra," the sweet, flowery voice said.

Sierra guessed who her visitor was right away. "Thanks. Tell him I'll be right there." Sierra hung up and said, "My brother is here. No doubt he's checking up on me again. You know, I thought it was going to be great having my big brother here so I could have someone to go to with all my problems, but if the rest of this year is anything like these first few days, the guy is going to drive me crazy!"

"Wes and you can get something to eat with Todd and me. Come on. Grab your key and let's go."

"My hair is still soaking!" Sierra said.

"It'll dry in two minutes outside," Christy said. "At least you smell good, which is a lot more than I can say for myself."

They hurried down the long hall and took the elevator to the main lobby area, where residents met their guests. The central lobby of Sierra's dorm, Sophia Hall, was as gorgeous as a tropical hotel lobby, with a court area in the center of the rectangular building. The large patio was paved with Tecate tiles, and the area was filled with trees and bushes, like a jungle. A number of benches were placed throughout, and a small fountain was located in the center.

Sierra looked around for Wes but didn't see him. Todd didn't appear to be anywhere visible, either.

"Knowing Todd, he's probably climbing one of the palm trees," Christy said, venturing into the arboretum area. Sierra followed her and noticed a guy walking around the backside of one of the trees as if he were examining it or trying to hide.

"What do you think?" Christy asked. "Is that one yours or mine?" All they could see was a bit of a gray T-shirt.

"Yours," Sierra guessed.

Then the guy rounded the tree, and they saw his face.

"Oh!" Christy whispered in surprise. "It's neither of ours."

"No," Sierra said slowly. "It's mine."

Christy reached for Sierra's arm. "Paul?" she whispered.

Instead of answering, Sierra found herself moving forward at the same pace Paul was moving toward her. He looked serious and had on his dirty work clothes, so Sierra guessed he had driven there right after a long, hot day of construction work.

"Hi," he said.

"Hi," Sierra answered.

Even sweaty and dirty he looked great. Sierra found it hard to slow down her heart enough for her to come up with some words. Paul looked past Sierra at Christy, and Sierra quickly introduced them, explaining that Christy was the friend Sierra had met in England and then later went with to Switzerland.

Paul nodded and said, "I've just come back from a year in Scotland."

"That's what Sierra told me."

Sierra could see Todd sneaking up behind Christy as she spoke. He had on a pale blue T-shirt that made his silver-blue eyes shout with mischief, but the finger to his lips told Sierra not to announce his approach. Paul played along as well, and before Christy knew what was happening, Todd stepped behind her and scooped her up in his arms.

She let out a startled squeal, which was overpowered by Todd announcing, "Me Tarzan, you . . . Hey, you not Jane!"

He put Christy down, and she looked at him with astonishment. "Todd, whatever got into you?"

"I've always wanted to do that," he said, returning to his easygoing manner. "Hey, Sierra. How's it going?"

Sierra introduced Paul, and the four of them stood there rather awkwardly.

"Do you want to get some dinner, Christy?" Todd asked.

"Sure," Christy said. She turned to Sierra and Paul.

"Would you guys like to join us?"

Paul and Sierra exchanged uncomfortable glances.

"I guess," Sierra finally said. She didn't know what to do.

"Actually," Paul said, "I'd like to talk with you, Sierra."

"Why don't you guys go ahead," Sierra said. "I'll see you later."

"Okay, later," Todd said. He gave Paul a chin-up nod and said, "See you around, Paul."

Paul nodded back, and Todd and Christy left, hand in hand. Sierra thought Todd had never seemed happier. And why not? He had Christy back and the "distance between them was a walking space." Sierra had hoped she and Paul would be that happy together, but all her feelings were so tied up in knots she didn't know if she could ever untangle them.

"I saw a bench back there," Paul said, motioning to where Sierra had first seen him behind the tree. "I was looking for a little more private place to talk." He walked into the center of the garden lobby and motioned for Sierra to follow him to a bench in the far right corner.

Sierra's mind raced with all the different directions this conversation might go. She could tell him that she had seen Jalene and their son and that he didn't have to hide that part of his life anymore. But then what would she say? That it didn't matter? That the two of them could go on and that she would be content to sit next to him on the "second step" and not go any further physically?

Right now Sierra wasn't sure she even wanted to be with Paul, let alone take any steps with him. It suddenly seemed ironic that after years of gaining a reputation around her friends as the "queen of confrontation," the last thing she wanted to do was have a heart-to-heart talk with Paul.

chapter sixteen

"**T**HIS IS A BEAUTIFUL PLACE," PAUL SAID AS HE sat on the bench and motioned for Sierra to sit next to him.

Sierra nodded her agreement.

"I can see why you said in your letters you liked this school so much. I'm even more interested in coming here now that I've seen the campus. It's very different from the University of Edinburgh." Paul was looking at her, but she was having a hard time looking at him.

"Sierra," Paul said, trying to get her full attention, "can you tell me what's going on?"

Sierra bit her lower lip.

"I don't understand why you didn't call me." Paul's voice was low and calm. "I know it wasn't the best timing on Sunday in the gym to try to talk about physical guidelines for our relationship, but I wanted you to know why I was spooked Saturday night. We were just getting too close too fast."

"I understand," Sierra said softly, looking down.

"Then why didn't you call me?"

"I wasn't ready to talk to you."

Paul balanced his arm on the back of the bench and

rested his unshaven cheek on his knuckles. "Why?"

Sierra knew this was the perfect opening to tell him that she knew about Jalene and the baby, but she couldn't do it. She couldn't say the words. Not used to being tongue-tied, she fingered the silver daffodil around her neck and wondered where all her boldness had gone.

"Listen," Paul said, reaching for one of her still-wet curls and gently brushing it off her shoulder. "Neither of us has told each other much about our past relationships."

Sierra turned to look at him, ready for his confession.

"And I just want to say that I realize you may have been more involved with guys in the past, so you're expecting more from me at this point. But I've set some pretty rigid standards for myself. Maybe we should have talked about that before we saw each other."

Sierra was startled. "You think I've been more involved with guys in the past?"

Paul's eyes showered her with understanding. "Hey, you don't have to tell me about any of that. I'm not your judge. I'm just saying you obviously were comfortable with a lot of physical expression the other night, but that's not the direction I'd like our relationship to go. That's why I thought we should pull back."

Sierra stared at Paul in disbelief. All she could do was repeat his statement. "You thought I was comfortable with a lot of physical expression?"

Paul nodded. "That might be what you're used to in relationships with other guys, but I want us to take it more slowly. That's what I've wanted from the beginning, which is why I suggested we write letters instead of E-mail. I'm not judging you for your past; I'm just saying this is how I'd like it to be for us."

Sierra sprang from the bench and said in angry disbelief, "You're not judging me?"

Paul stood, too, caught off guard by her reaction.

Before Sierra could blurt out that she was as pure and innocent as a lamb and that Paul was the only guy with whom she had ever expressed the kinds of physical affection she gave him the other night, two girls walked in their direction, talking loudly. Paul and Sierra stood frozen, staring at each other, waiting for the girls to pass.

Sierra's startled anger overtook any sense of reason, and she blurted out, "You're a fine one to be going around overlooking my past! What about your past?"

Paul looked stunned. "What about my past?" His voice was rising to meet the intensity of Sierra's.

"Jalene and you."

"What about Jalene and me?"

"Oh, come on, Paul. You kept it from me all this time. But then I saw her last week, and I figured it out."

"Figured what out?"

"I saw him, Paul. I saw him with Jalene, and I figured out why you wanted to go to Portland last June."

"I wanted to go to Portland to see you," Paul said loudly.

"And a few other people so you could make things right with them. Isn't that what you said?"

Paul still looked frustrated and confused. "What are you getting at, Sierra? This is making no sense."

"Oh, it's not?"

"No," Paul said, lowering his voice. "It's not. Can you just tell me what you're trying to say?"

"Okay, I'll tell you. It's Jalene," Sierra said, looking at him like an eager lawyer making her closing statements to the jury. "Jalene and the *baby*." She gave extra emphasis to the last word, raising her eyebrows in a knowing expression. "And since you didn't tell me and I had to figure it out myself, well, to be honest with you, I haven't quite decided where my trust level is in this relationship at the moment. I thought you—"

"You thought what?" Paul cut her off, his arms folded across his chest.

"I thought—"

"You thought the kid you saw with Jalene was mine?" Paul's face was turning red.

Sierra folded her arms, too, and stood her ground. "I'm not saying I'm judging your past in any way. But it sure would have been nice if I'd heard it from you first."

"Listen, Sierra," he stated, "you didn't hear it from me first because there was nothing for you to hear. I don't know whose baby Jalene had when you saw her, and I don't know what she told you, but there's no way it's mine. Absolutely no way! It's not possible."

"It's not?"

"No! And I can't believe you assumed it could be, Sierra! How could you have jumped to such conclusions?"

Instead of meekly apologizing at the revelation, Sierra let her nervous fury fly. "And what is it you assumed about me? Just a few minutes ago you said you thought I was comfortable with a lot of physical expression because that must be what I was used to. Well, guess again, Paul! There haven't been any other guys—ever. Not even one."

His expression softened. "What about Randy?"

"Randy is my buddy."

"What about that guy you told me you met in Switzerland?"

"Alex?" Sierra laughed. "He hugged me good-bye at the airport by pressing his cheek against mine. How's that for physical intimacy?"

"And there hasn't been anyone else?"

"Well, let's see, there was Drake. He put his arm around me once when we were walking the dog together. Oh, and he held my hand when he prayed with me one time in the car."

Paul rubbed his neck as if he were trying to relax his thick muscles.

"Paul," Sierra railed, still fired up, "you are looking at one of the world's oldest pair of virgin lips! They've been on my face for almost 18 years and have only been used to kiss the cheeks of grandmothers, the feet of infants, and Brutus."

"Brutus?"

"Our dog."

"Oh" was all Paul said. Sierra's ravings seemed to have calmed him down a bit. "I misunderstood," he said. "The way you were coming on to me Saturday night, I assumed you were much more experienced."

Something inside of Sierra went *Twang!* "The way I was coming on to you!" she yelled. "I can't believe you're saying that! You were the one who took me down to the beach and held me in that little cave and quoted me your poetry. Are you telling me that's not coming on to me?"

"Is that what you thought I was doing?"

"I thought you were treating me the way you would treat your girlfriend."

"And what were you doing?" Paul asked.

"I was treating you the way I'd treat my boyfriend. My

first boyfriend in my whole life, I might add, not that that matters at this point."

Paul rubbed his neck again. "Is that what we are? Are you saying we're now boyfriend and girlfriend? Are we a couple, Sierra?" Paul looked at her, his jaw clenched, his blue-gray eyes clouding over, waiting for her answer.

chapter seventeen

SIERRA CROSSED HER ARMS AROUND HER MIDDLE, TRY-ing to keep her upset stomach from grumbling loud enough for Paul to hear. "I don't know," she answered with her chin held up defiantly. "You tell me. What are we?"

"I don't know," Paul said, folding his arms across his chest. "And maybe I don't want to feel pressured to figure it out right now."

"Who's pressuring you?" Sierra said. "Certainly not me."

"That's right," Paul said, slapping his forehead with the palm of his hand as an exaggerated gesture. "You're not pressuring me. As a matter of fact, you're not even calling me when I ask you. So I have to wonder what's wrong and rush up here from work so I can find out. And here you are, dreaming up some promiscuous past life for me!"

Sierra had a half an impulse to apologize and admit she had been wrong to jump to conclusions. But she couldn't let herself. It still bothered her that he had jumped to conclusions about her as well. "Oh yeah? Well, what about the promiscuous past life you dreamed up about me? Or doesn't that count?"

Before Paul could answer, Katie appeared. "Hi, kids!" she called across the courtyard. "Did Todd and Christy leave already to go eat? Hey, you must be Paul." Katie gave him a friendly punch on the shoulder. "I was wondering when I'd get to meet you. Sierra has told me all about you."

"Really?" Paul said, looking at Sierra and then back at Katie. "And did she tell you about a certain baby boy in Portland who is supposedly my son?"

Katie looked at Paul. Her clear green eyes showed sincere compassion. She nodded and said, "And you know what I told Sierra? I told her, 'Big whoop.' What's past is past. As long as everything is settled between God and you, then it's time to move on, right?"

Paul hesitated only a moment before saying, "Right. Time to move on." He shot a pain-filled expression at Sierra and said calmly, "You know what? I don't think I can do this." He brushed passed her and headed straight for the door.

Sierra felt her heart pounding in her throat. Everything inside her told her to run after him, but she couldn't move a muscle.

"Was it something I said?" Katie asked. "If it was, I'm sorry."

"No, it was me. I messed up, Katie. I messed up bad! Paul and Jalene never had a baby. I jumped to all the wrong conclusions. I should never have said anything to you or Christy."

"Then go tell him that," Katie said, motioning in the direction Paul had gone.

"I can't. It's too messed up. And I'm still mad at him. He assumed I had a very active past, too. He thinks I'm pressuring him to be my boyfriend or something." Sierra sank onto the bench, her arms still folded tightly across her stomach. "I think I'm going to be sick."

"Hey, don't get sick here," Katie said, pulling Sierra up by the arm. "You should go back to your room. I'll go talk to Paul."

"No, Katie, don't."

"Hey, it's the least I can do after what happened. You go back to your room, and I'll call you, okay? I need to apologize to Paul." Katie was already moving away from Sierra as she said the last sentence. "I have to run if I'm going to catch him." With that, she sprinted toward the front doors.

Sierra called out to Katie one more time before giving up and heading to her room. With each step, she remembered vividly Paul's assumptions of her, and her hurt and frustration fanned the fire that had not yet died down inside.

Stomping down the hall, Sierra entered her room and slammed the door behind her—something she was never allowed to do at home. That particular habit had been curbed when she was a small child and she would throw what her mother called "dramatic displays of independence."

Sierra certainly was in the mood to throw one of those "dramatic displays" right now, and no one was there to stop her. Or discipline her. Or listen to her. Or comfort her. She was all alone.

Sierra picked up one of her throw pillows and threw it at the wall. That didn't do any good, so she began pacing back and forth, trying to make sense of everything, picking out each feeling and trying to identify it.

First, she knew she felt remorse over her assumption

that Paul and Jalene had had a child. Her imagination had gotten way out of control on that one. Why hadn't she listened to Wes or Christy when they tried to get her to look at other possible explanations? Why did she always get carried away with her zealous, impulsive assumptions? She didn't blame Paul for being mad at her. He had every right to be furious. If he never spoke to her again, she wouldn't blame him.

But then, her other feeling was anger at Paul because he had made assumptions about her, too. And that wasn't fair. Those assumptions hurt her more than she would have expected.

And why did Paul have to walk away from the problem? Why couldn't he have stayed so they could fight it out? Sierra almost always preferred a good fight to silence.

But then she recalled Paul's red face and arms folded across his chest. That image made her smile against her will. *So the man's got fire in his spirit,* she thought.

She had never seen that side of him. Some things don't come up in written words, even after dozens of letters. The maddening thing was, Paul's ability to communicate so clearly what he was thinking and feeling only made Sierra adore him more than ever. She knew she could never love or respect a guy who couldn't match her zeal. And she certainly didn't want to end up with a guy who would let her bulldoze him with fiery words. That revelation acted as cool water, quenching the fire within her.

Sierra lifted the silver daffodil from the end of the chain around her neck and pressed the cool metal to her lips. *Oh Paul, I'm sorry. Please come back. I want to apologize. Father God, can't You make him come back? I can't let the sun go down on my anger. I need to make things right with Paul.*

In the silence, Sierra thought, waited, and prayed. When Katie didn't call, Sierra decided to ease her loneliness by eating a granola bar and drinking some apple juice. It proved an unsatisfying solution.

Just as she was about to start in on a second granola bar, she heard a knock on her door. It was Katie, and she was shaking her head.

"I couldn't find him. He must have parked out front and taken off immediately. I'm sorry, Sierra. I've been thinking about all this, and I really feel bad. I never should have jumped to those conclusions about Paul without all the facts."

"I know," Sierra said. "But it's my fault, not yours. It was my assumption, not yours."

Katie flopped onto Vicki's empty bed and lay on her back, staring at the ceiling. "Have you prayed about everything yet?"

"Yes."

"And what do you think you should do?"

"I don't know. I want to talk to him."

"We could take Baby Hummer and go down to Paul's house in San Diego, or you could borrow Baby Hummer and go by yourself." Katie turned on her side and faced Sierra, who was sitting tensely on the edge of her bed.

"I don't know where his house is. Maybe I could call Tawni and ask her for dirctions."

"Do you have the address?" Katie asked. "We could look it up on the Internet."

"What if he calls here?" Sierra said. "What if he drives

halfway home and calms down the way I have? What if he comes back here or calls?"

"I could get on the computer in the library, and you could wait here," Katie suggested.

"You would do that for me?" Sierra asked.

"Are you kidding? As the last honorary member of the P.O. Club, I find it my duty to serve former members whenever the opportunity arises."

It took Sierra a moment to remember what Katie was referring to. When she did, she smiled. "Oh, right, our little 'Pals Only Club' we dreamed up in England. You and I vowed to be only pals with guys so we wouldn't have to experience all the emotional trauma our friends were going through with their boyfriends." Sierra felt a little sad as she said, "Looks as though I might be back in the club after I talk to Paul. That is, if he still wants to even be friends with me."

"He will," Katie said confidently. "When I saw him standing there next to you, I immediately knew who he was, and honestly, my first thought was that you two look like you belong together."

"Why do you say that?"

"You just do. Some couples match. You know, like Doug and Tracy, and Christy and Todd. Paul and you go together."

Sierra let out a sigh. "Yeah, well, we'll see."

chapter eighteen

A FEW MINUTES AFTER KATIE LEFT THE ROOM, THE phone rang. For half a second, Sierra considered not answering it. *That'll show him,* she thought defiantly. *He thinks I'm waiting for him to call.* But Sierra had never been good at playing hard to get, so she lunged for the receiver on the second ring.

"Good, you're there," the male voice said on the other end.

Sierra sighed. "I'm not interested in getting something to eat, if that's what you're going to ask, Wesley."

"No, I'm not offering food. I want to ask a favor."

"Well, what is it? This is kind of a bad time."

"I want to know if you would go to the chapel in about 10 minutes."

"Why?"

There was a pause. "This is really important, Sierra. I have rarely asked you to do anything for me. I'm asking that, just this once, you do something for me without all the details up front. All you have to do is say yes or no. Can you go to the prayer chapel in about 10 minutes?"

Sierra drew in a deep breath. "Oh, all right." She figured that by the time she had completed this silly secret mission of Wesley's and returned to her room, Katie would be back with the map. If Paul did call while she was gone, he would leave a message for her, and she could call him back and talk to him with a much calmer spirit. "I'll be there in 10 minutes, Wesley."

"That's great. Thanks, Sierra."

She hung up the phone and gave herself a quick look in the mirror. Her hair had dried during her "heated" discussion with Paul. Her black eye had toned down some, and none of her previous fiery or queasy feelings now showed in her skin tone. She scribbled a quick note to Katie, grabbed her room key, and left the note on her door.

As Sierra hiked across campus, she figured out Wes wanted to meet with her to instruct her not to jump to conclusions about Paul. The prayer chapel was probably the most private place on campus. If her brother was going to lecture her, it might as well be in private. Well, she had news for him. She had already figured out she shouldn't jump to conclusions. What she hadn't quite figured out was how to make peace with Paul. She hoped Wes would be in an extra-understanding mood when she told him everything, and he would be able to give her some advice.

Sierra thought it was ironic that now she wanted her brother's advice. It made her realize how much her opinions had been swinging back and forth the past few days. If this was all part of getting used to being on her own and charting her way through her relationship with Paul, then Sierra hoped she could find some calm middle ground soon.

Rancho Corona's campus covered nearly 20 acres on the top of a mesa. The prayer chapel was on the southwest corner of the mesa, and the walk there, in the cool of the evening, refreshed Sierra. She thought of how the Bible talked about the Lord God walking with Adam and Eve in the Garden of Eden in the cool of the evening. It made her wonder what that must have been like, to walk and talk with God. Then it struck her that the same God who went walking with the first woman was still here, invisibly walking beside her, down this trail past the large meadow.

Sierra impulsively began to talk with God aloud. "I guess Paul and I aren't the first man and woman to have a conflict, are we?" she said. "Not that it's a good thing, but it's not unusual, is it?"

Only the evening breeze answered her with soothing strokes across her cheeks. Suddenly Sierra realized that her most important relationship was with God. He would never leave her. He would never make incorrect assumptions about her because He already knew everything. He would never give up on His relationship with her because He had promised in His Word that His love for her was forever.

Picking up her pace, Sierra felt eager to reach the prayer chapel. She wanted to have time to kneel and pray in that quiet, holy place before Wes arrived. She wanted to reaffirm her commitment to Christ and ceremoniously surrender her relationship with Paul. An urgency seemed to envelop her, and when she turned onto the path that led to the chapel, the wind seemed to push her forward, into the chapel's sanctuary.

Opening the door cautiously and peering inside, Sierra was glad to see no one was there. She tiptoed up to the altar at the front of the chapel and got down on her knees, folding her hands to pray. Above the altar was a stained glass window that bore the emblem of the ranch that had occupied this mesa years ago. It was a gold crown with a cross coming out of the center of it at a slant. She bowed her head and noticed how the evening sunlight spilled through the golden glass that formed the crown and settled in a shining circle around Sierra's heart.

She closed her eyes and prayed in a whisper, "Lord God, thank You so much for bringing me here to Rancho. I want to honor You with my life. I want what You want for the relationships in my life, especially with Paul. God, forgive me for messing things up, and please give us a fresh start. I don't know how to do this boyfriend-girlfriend thing. Will You teach me? I want to trust You in every way with every area of my life. I love You, Jesus."

With her whispered "Amen," Sierra heard the chapel's door open, and she wondered if she should jump up before Wes saw her kneeling at the altar. But it didn't matter to her. She had just shared a meaningful moment with the same Lord God who had walked with Eve in the garden. Sierra had no reason to run and hide the way Eve had when she disobeyed. Sierra had been forgiven. She knew it. She could face God and Wes without shame.

Sierra didn't turn to look at her brother. Instead, she listened as his footsteps approached. She wanted to linger one more moment, gazing at the light coming through the stained glass window and reveling in the fresh, clean feeling that had come over her.

She felt her brother's hand on her shoulder and impulsively pressed her cheek against it. Then with a quick kiss on his knuckle, she said, "I know what you're going to say."

"Oh, do you?" the voice behind her answered. But it wasn't Wesley's voice.

Sierra froze.

Paul knelt beside her. She slowly turned her head to look at him, all her defenses down. "I'm sorry," she said, the instant her eyes met his.

"I'm sorry, too. I'm not sure what happened," Paul said. "But instead of leaving, I decided to talk to your brother, and I'm glad I did."

Sierra noticed Paul had on a clean shirt. It was one of Wesley's new, short-sleeved, blue cotton shirts. Paul smelled fresh, too. He obviously had calmed down— maybe in a cold shower—and was ready to talk the way Sierra was.

"You know what I think?" Paul said.

Sierra waited for him to go on.

"I think we got off track. I'd like to get back on track."

"I would, too," Sierra said. "Only now I understand I had way too many expectations and assumptions."

"I did, too," Paul said. "Can we start again and take it nice and slow?"

Sierra nodded.

"I need to apologize for not communicating more clearly before we went for our walk on the beach. I realize I was being very familiar with you physically. That's why I was trying to say I didn't want our relationship to go in that direction. It could become an expectation that every time we see each other we have to hold hands or whatever just to keep the relationship at the same level. Does that make sense?"

"Yes," Sierra said, adjusting her position so now she was sitting on the floor in front of the altar.

"I've written out these verses I found in First Thessa-lonians." Paul settled in on the floor across from her. They both were speaking in hushed tones and using tender expressions, a vast difference from their earlier confrontation. He pulled a folded piece of paper from his back pocket and said, "This is what I want for our relationship."

He read the first eight verses of chapter four quickly, and Sierra asked him to go back and read part of it again.

" '. . . For God wants you to be holy and pure, and to keep clear of all sexual sin so that each of you will marry in holiness and honor.' " Paul looked at Sierra and said, "I don't know whose wife you're going to be someday, but I don't want to dishonor that guy, whoever he is, or you, by taking anything that is meant for him alone."

Sierra felt her heart melting into a little puddle.

"So I don't want to take advantage of you by becoming too physically involved."

"You know what, Paul? I don't want to take advantage of you either. And I don't want to steal anything that belongs to your future wife. But I have to tell you something: I really pay attention to your words. What you say to me or write to me is how I gauge our relationship. So if you write incredible poems just for me, I'm thinking our relationship is deepening. Your poems may be saying more to me than you mean for them to."

"I didn't realize that."

"I know you've been careful with your words to me in your letters, but I have to tell you, your words capture my heart."

Paul nodded his understanding. "I guess that's similar to how it was for me when we were on the beach and you were so free with your physical expressions. I think I took it to mean more than it was."

Sierra shrugged. "I'm a rookie at this. Now I know not to be so expressive."

"And I'll watch my words."

Paul reached out and, touching the silver daffodil around Sierra's neck, said, "But don't go too far the other way and clam up, Sierra. I've always admired your zealous spirit. I like the way you openly and honestly express yourself."

"But it wouldn't hurt if I tried to control that zeal a little more, right?"

Paul tilted his head. "Maybe. And I need to control my poetic spirit, right?"

"Maybe," Sierra said, smiling at him. "So, where do we go from here?"

"I think I know," Paul said, letting go of the necklace and holding out his hand, inviting her to take it. Sierra slipped her hand into his, and Paul held it lightly. He looked at the blue and amber hues of the stained glass windows that were sprinkled across their hands. "We just keep going from here, helping each other learn how to live controlled lives of sanctification and honor."

"And lives that are a little more balanced," Sierra said, thinking of how much she had been swinging emotionally back and forth the last few days.

"Balanced," Paul repeated. "And since the next chapter in First Thessalonians says to greet one another with a holy kiss, here's my answer to that balance." Paul lifted her hand to his lips. With hushed words, he said, "This is from my heart to yours. A holy kiss for the Daffodil Queen." Paul tenderly kissed the top of Sierra's hand as only a romantic poet would.

She smiled, repressing the impulse to throw her arms

around his neck and return his kiss on his lips. To her surprise, Sierra found she could sit there, without having to act on the impulse. She remembered Christy's story about the piggy bank, and Sierra secretly decided that she had just saved a very huge kiss for her future husband in her invisible piggy bank.

"You interested in getting some dinner?" Paul asked.

"Sure," Sierra said, feeling settled and at peace about where their relationship was and where it was headed.

Paul stood and offered her his hand to pull her up. She rose, and together they left the quiet chapel. The air around them seemed charged with a holy presence. Sierra imagined that Adam and Eve must have experienced the same somber stillness when the Lord God walked with them in the cool of the evening.

"He's here, you know," Sierra said to Paul.

"I know," Paul said.

They paused just long enough to watch the bright orange September sun dip into the horizon. Then, circled by the golden light of God's presence and His promise, Paul and Sierra walked side by side along the trail that led toward the campus and on toward their future.

Two Captivating Series from Robin Jones Gunn

THE CHRISTY MILLER SERIES

1 • Summer Promise
2 • A Whisper and a Wish
3 • Yours Forever
4 • Surprise Endings
5 • Island Dreamer
6 • A Heart Full of Hope
7 • True Friends
8 • Starry Night
9 • Seventeen Wishes
10 • A Time to Cherish
11 • Sweet Dreams
12 • A Promise Is Forever

THE SIERRA JENSEN SERIES

1 • Only You, Sierra
2 • In Your Dreams
3 • Don't You Wish
4 • Close Your Eyes
5 • Without a Doubt
6 • With This Ring
7 • Open Your Heart
8 • Time Will Tell
9 • Now Picture This
10 • Hold On Tight
11 • Closer Than Ever
12 • Take My Hand

FOCUS ON THE FAMILY®
LIKE THIS BOOK?

Then you'll love *Brio* magazine! Written especially for teen girls, it's packed each month with 32 pages on everything from fiction and faith to fashion, food . . . even guys! Best of all, it's all from a Christian perspective! But don't just take our word for it. Instead, see for yourself by requesting a complimentary copy.

Simply write Focus on the Family, Colorado Springs, CO 80995 (in Canada, write P.O. Box 9800, Stn. Terminal, Vancouver, B.C. V6B 4G3) and mention that you saw this offer in the back of this book. You may also call 1-800-232-6459 (in Canada, call 1-800-661-9800).

You may also visit our Web site (www.family.org) to learn more about the ministry or find out if there is a Focus on the Family office in your country.

Want to become everyone's favorite baby-sitter? Then *The Ultimate Baby-Sitter's Survival Guide* is for you! It's packed with page after page of practical information and ways to stay in control; organize mealtime, bath time and bedtime; and handle emergency situations. It also features an entire section of safe, creative and downright crazy indoor and outdoor activities that will keep kids challenged, entertained and away from the television. Easy-to-read and reference, it's the ideal book for providing the best care to children, earning money and having fun at the same time.

Call Focus on the Family at the number above, or check out your local Christian bookstore.

Focus on the Family is an organization that is dedicated to helping you and your family establish lasting, loving relationships with each other and the Lord. It's why we exist! If we can assist you or your family in any way, please feel free to contact us. We'd love to hear from you!